"Will You Let Go of Me . . . !"

Even as she said it, she was trying to
squirm out of his grasp. His clasp loosened
slightly but not enough for her to free
herself. "Nobody told me you had such
a nasty temper," he said thoughtfully.
Then, without a wasted motion, she was
pulled against his tall frame so fast that
she gasped. When she started to protest,
her chin was tilted up and secured in a
firm grip. Then, with every evidence of
masculine enjoyment, his mouth came
down to cover hers. And Cristina's
emotions exploded like a fireworks
display on the Fourth of July. . . .

"Beware the fury of a patient man."

Chapter One

◆◆◆◆◆◆◆◆◆◆◆◆◆◆◆◆◆◆◆◆◆◆◆◆◆◆◆◆

There was no getting around it, Cristina decided—it was going to be one of those days.

When she'd gotten up that morning, there had been no intimation of trouble brewing at the mountain resort she called home. Her automatic glance from the bedroom window revealed that the sun was pale but determined as it illuminated the fantastic scenery in front of her. The ruggedly beautiful slopes of Mount Rainier looked as if they'd been sculpted by Michelangelo especially for the occasion, with the mammoth white glaciers contrasting sharply against the cloudless sky.

Cristina's glance swept downward, admiring the different shades of green on the alpine growth which dotted the lower meadows and, still closer, the varied colors of wild flowers on the plateau above the lodge.

That venerable structure fitted easily into the rustic framework of northwest scenery. It was a steep-roofed building of weathered cedar which took on a patina of silver with the dew of early morning. Lightning rods topped the chimneys for the massive stone fireplaces at either end of the four-storied complex. The spacious lobby on the ground floor was the communal gathering place, with the dining room and gift shop nearby. The next two floors were reserved for guests, and the dormer-windowed quarters on the fourth floor housed most of the lodge staff.

Cristina herself had spent one summer on that floor four years before, when she'd worked as a receptionist at the lodge during a college vacation. In those days, very few of the staff knew that Andrew Kelly, manager and part-owner of the resort who lived in a chalet on the grounds, was also her grandfather. Lincoln Murray, his partner, lived in San Francisco and was content to leave the running of the property in Andrew Kelly's capable hands. Two years later, Murray had died, leaving his share of the lodge to his only daughter, Regina. She conferred with Andrew Kelly about the running of the resort, and the two of them had decided managerial tasks should be handled by a California firm which specialized in such things.

Two more years passed before Andrew issued a call for help, asking his granddaughter to join the lodge's staff as an assistant manager.

Unfortunately, there had barely been time for Cris to learn of his uneasiness about recent happenings at the property before he'd succumbed to pneumonia following minor surgery.

Cristina had tried to carry on without showing how much she missed the kindly old gentleman, but even two months later she felt his presence—especially in the chalet which she now occupied when she finished her duties at the lodge. As days passed in uneventful fashion, however, she began to suspect that her grandfather's conviction about a Kelly being needed on the lodge premises was simply an elderly man's whim.

She was thinking about it that morning as she locked the chalet door behind her and walked to work along the path leading to the lodge. A young Japanese man weeding a flower bed at the edge of the parking lot caught her attention and she pulled up beside his crouched figure. "Good morning, Kazy. You're starting awfully early. At this rate, you'll be finished before noon."

He grinned approvingly at her trim outfit of white slacks and sweater topped with a yellow wool shirt. "That's the whole idea, Miss Kelly—ma'am. I've asked for the afternoon off, and Mr. Brock will be out here checking to see if I've finished."

"Mr. Brock's a very conscientious manager," she said, trying to keep a straight face. "You'd better watch out—he could send his assistant, and she's even worse on inspection tours."

Kazy's grin broadened. "I'll chance it. If you get any official complaints, I'll defend you."

"When you hang out your shingle after the bar exam, I'll take you up on that. And you can stop looking over your shoulder, because there's nobody around to overhear," Cristina assured him. "Honestly—anybody would think you were covering up a criminal record or something. I've never understood why you're so secretive about studying law."

"Because Mr. Brock wouldn't have hired me in the first place if he'd known. Gardeners are supposed to be gardeners—not Perry Masons on the side. He didn't have any problems when you came to work here. You'd had some hotel experience, so you fitted right in."

"Not much experience," Cris said, remembering that early summer when she'd been full of youthful enthusiasms. She smiled ruefully as she thought about it. "Actually I didn't learn very much."

"Something must have penetrated," Kazy said,

his oriental features impassive. "Of course, it didn't hurt that you had red hair."

"Reddish-brown," she corrected.

"Red," he persisted, and peered at her near-sightedly. "And green eyes plus all the assets to go with them. A man notices these things."

"Yoshi might not approve of your survey," Cristina said, smiling despite herself. "Aren't engaged men supposed to confine their observations to their fiancées?"

"I'll look at her this afternoon if I ever get this weeding done," Kazy said, with a sigh. "She's changed shifts to be off with me so we can hike down to the lakes."

"Does Mr. Brock know?"

"I don't think so." Kazy looked perturbed. "It won't matter, will it? We've been trying to get some time off together all week."

"It'll be fine. I'll check as soon as I get to the lodge and make sure the schedules are all covered. The lakes region might be a good hike for those Swedish engineers and their wives who are coming next week," she went on, thinking aloud. "We could serve a trail lunch at Reflection Cove."

Kazy nodded, his quick mind following her thoughts. "I'll do a rough time check today if you want. Better still, if you sent a box lunch with Yoshi, we could research every angle of the tour."

"That's blackmail, counselor, but I'll see what I can do. It certainly sounds like more fun than staying behind a desk." She started on toward the lodge, saying over her shoulder, "If you aren't careful, you'll end up with a chaperone, too."

Kazy waved good-naturedly and bent to his weeding again.

On most mornings, the wide flagstone terrace of

the lodge would have been deserted, with any activity centered in the dining room instead. This day, Cristina discovered Tom Warden, the lodge accountant, bending over a pile of luggage which included a backpack, sleeping bag, and a good-sized leather suitcase stacked by the front door.

"What in the world's going on?" Cris asked when she came up to him.

"That's what I'd like to know," he said as he straightened. "I was walking in the door minding my own business when this fellow drove up and started unloading a station wagon. I tried to tell him that he couldn't go off and leave his stuff untended while he parked."

"Why didn't you call a bellboy?" Cristina asked, finally managing to get a word in edgeways.

Tom's thin lips settled into an aggrieved line. "Because there wasn't one to call. Brock won't be happy when he learns about that. I know you don't like to put one of your kids on report, Cristina, but it's time some of them learned a sense of responsibility."

Cristina tried to ignore her feeling of impending disaster. "There's no need to tell Mr. Brock anything until I find out what happened." She gestured toward the luggage. "When is the man coming back?"

"I didn't ask." It didn't take the tone of his voice to tell that he was annoyed by her refusal to match his indignation. A scowl marred his normally earnest features, and Cris knew he didn't like the day's usual pattern disturbed. He was a tall young man in his late twenties, undistinguished except for his determination to get ahead in the California-based management firm that operated the lodge. He had all the patience in the world with a set of figures, but he displayed a short temper when confronted with human errors. It was not a quality that endeared him to the rest of the staff. Cris was aware of this and tried doubly hard to keep her own annoyance under control.

"Well, we can't leave the things here," she began, and bent down to pick up the suitcase.

"I'll get it," Tom said, putting out a hand to stop her. "It's just the principle of the thing. He had no right abandoning his stuff on the doorstep."

"However, he *did* have a right to expect a bellhop here to receive it." Cris went ahead to open the heavy lodge door and watched Tom drop the belongings by the empty bell captain's desk. "Thanks very much for helping."

"It's okay." He was brushing a pine needle from the sleeve of his sport coat. "I won't say anything to Brock this time, but you'd better sort things out. The trouble is you're too easy with these kids." With that pronouncement, he strode off toward his office, passing the reception desk where Yoshi was watching covertly.

"I told Jimmy he'd get into trouble if he disappeared," the petite Japanese girl said when Cristina approached. "Sometimes I think Mr. Warden is even worse than Mr. Brock when it comes to fussing."

"In this case, I'm on their side. Why in the dickens isn't Jimmy on duty? Did he oversleep again?"

Yoshi nodded with some reluctance. "He's down in the kitchen having coffee to wake up."

"I can take care of that," Cris said somewhat grimly as she turned toward the closed glass doors of the dining room. "If he'd stop trying to act like a Casanova in his spare time, he could manage to work an early morning shift." She paused with her hand on the door. "How many guests are checking in this morning?"

Yoshi frowned as she ran her finger down the reservations log. "No one special for an early arrival. Why? Are you wondering who that luggage belongs to?"

"I guess so. We'll find out eventually. By the way, I saw Kazy outside—he mentioned that you were going out this afternoon. Did you find someone to cover for you?"

Yoshi's pale cheeks took on a twinge of color and she ran nervous fingers through her cap of black hair. "I hope so . . . it's almost certain."

Cris managed to stifle a groan that threatened to become audible. "Okay," she said finally. "There shouldn't be any problem then."

"Don't worry," Yoshi said; "I won't pull the same trick Jimmy did."

Cristina smiled and started toward the dining room wing. "Believe me, he won't try it again after I find him. See you later."

The young bellboy wasn't hard to locate since he was leaning against a counter in the kitchen at that moment, chatting with the short-order chef while they both drank coffee. It took only Cristina's uplifted eyebrows and her quiet comment that she'd like to see him later for him to quickly swallow the last of his coffee and beat a hasty retreat toward the lobby.

"I told him he'd get in the soup if he hung around here," the chef said cheerfully.

"Not literally, I hope," Cris replied. "How's everything on the food front?"

"Can't complain." The man settled his tall white hat more firmly on his head. " 'Cept about that new order of potatoes that came in late yesterday.

They're not the top-grade Idahos we ordered. Take a look, Miss Kelly, and see if you don't agree with me. The bags are still out on the porch."

"I'm sure you're right." She started toward the rear door of the kitchen, where orders were stacked until they were approved. "We'll have to ask if they can deliver another shipment before the weekend. Otherwise, we'll need to send a truck down."

"It's a nuisance, all right," he agreed. "Maybe we can make do with these. See what you think."

Cris nodded and opened the door to the porch. She slit the lacing on a produce sack and ran her hand through the top layer of potatoes. There were all sizes and shapes in the bag—certainly not the premium baking variety the chef needed. She pulled the bag back together and dusted her hands.

Frowning, she walked over to the porch railing. The eastern sky was alight with color as the sun continued to climb, and only a few tailings of morning mist lingered on the mountainside, promising another clear August day. Most any other time, Chris would have noted it happily, but just then she was trying to visualize the day's work schedule, ignoring her certainty that Kazy would be the man she'd normally choose for the trip to the produce wholesaler.

"Damn!" Cristina said softly to herself as she wondered how she could salvage Kazy and Yoshi's hopes for the afternoon and keep the kitchen supplied as well. "Damn!" she said again and decided to follow Jimmy's example and see if a cup of coffee would solve her problems.

She was just turning toward the kitchen door when a station wagon pulled up by the loading area below the porch. Cris watched, her frown deepening, as the driver turned off his engine and got out of the car. He reached back to get a light-blue linen blazer before rolling the car window down partway and then closing the door.

He was a lean and rangy individual with thick dark hair and a tanned skin. Cris noticed the tan especially because of the contrast with his white oxford-cloth shirt. An instant later she became conscious of his broad shoulders when he shrugged into the blue blazer and absently tightened his tie. He had started up the drive toward the front of the lodge before Cristina suddenly came to her senses and called to him over the porch railing. "Hey, you can't leave that station wagon there!"

The man turned and squinted against the sun as he searched the porch to locate her, his jaw tight with annoyance.

Cris went on, softening her edict. "Guests aren't allowed to park back here. There should be plenty of space out front in our regular lot this early in the morning."

His gaze had found her by then, but he took his time as he fished a pair of sunglasses from his jacket pocket and put them on. "There might be plenty of space, but there isn't any shade."

"Well, I'm sorry, but that doesn't change things. This is our delivery zone and I can't make any exceptions. You can understand that, I'm sure."

He continued to stare up at her, but if he was impressed by her smile and courteous voice, there was no indication of it. He simply went on in the same implacable tone. "I can understand it but I doubt if Tessa would. Her tongue's hanging out already. I was just coming in to get her a drink."

The sudden appearance of an Irish setter

pressing her nose against a rear window of the station wagon established beyond the shadow of a doubt who Tessa was. Cristina clutched the porch railing, overcoming an impulse to hold her head instead. "I'm sorry about this, Mr. . . ."

"Colby. Webb Colby."

"Mr. Colby," she acknowledged. "Someone should have told you that we don't allow dogs in the lodge."

"I'm aware of that. I read the brochure that came along with my reservation confirmation, Miss . . ."

"Kelly, Cristina Kelly," she said, sure that he'd framed his response so that she'd have to follow his lead. "I'm the assistant manager here."

"Fine." His voice was terse. "This is within your province then. The dog belongs to a friend of mine who's due in on the Skyline Trail this morning with a hiking party. I promised that Tessa would be waiting for him. You can't expect me to keep the dog shut in a parked car with the sun beating on the roof."

"No, of course not." Cristina bit her lip. "But honestly, you can't leave the station wagon there. The fire marshall will object if no one else does."

"What do you suggest I do?"

There was an undercurrent of amusement in his words that made color blaze in her cheeks.

"If you'll pull around to the side entrance and park while you register, you can take the dog up to your room afterward. I'll tell the floor maid that it's all right," she said, sounding stiffer than usual because somehow he'd put her on the defensive since the moment she'd hailed him.

"That's very nice of you." Webb walked back toward the station wagon, and the setter's tail started waving as he approached. He reached through the open car window to pat the dog's head and then glanced at Cris again. "How do I reach this side entrance you're talking about?"

"Go back the way you came and make a left turn by the end of the parking lot where the sign says 'Employees Only.' I'll open the fire door on that wing of the lodge so you can bring the dog in that way." As she saw his eyes narrow consideringly, she added with some impatience, "I wish you'd hurry. It's still early and there aren't many guests around."

"And you prefer it that way?"

"I certainly do. The manager would have my head for this. It's not only against lodge rules—he's allergic to dogs. He starts sneezing when one even walks by."

"Then Tessa will have to get under cover in a hurry. I'll come back to the front desk as soon as I can," Webb promised as he slid his long length under the steering wheel.

Cristina watched him turn the station wagon and accelerate along the drive toward the parking lot before she went back through the kitchen door. She was breathing hard and saw with some surprise that her fingers were trembling when she stopped by the coffee urn and poured herself a mug of coffee.

The short-order chef watched with interest. "Having your coffee break early today, aren't you?"

She tried to sound nonchalant. "Jimmy gave me the idea, and the way things are going, I'll be back for a second cup."

As she started carrying it toward the dining room, he hailed her before she'd taken more than a few steps. "Miss Kelly, what about those potatoes?"

"Potatoes?" Then she grimaced apologetically. "Oh, *those* potatoes. You were absolutely right about them. I'll get them replaced."

"We'll need the others by dinner," he warned. "Dinner tonight."

She nodded. "You'll have new potatoes by dinner tonight if I have to drive the truck down myself and pick them up."

And I might just have to do that very thing, she announced to the empty lobby as she closed the dining room door behind her and walked back to the reception desk. She was relieved to see that Yoshi was still the only person in sight. Cristina put her coffee mug down on the polished wooden counter and said, "Mr. Colby has arrived. He's parking his car at the moment, but he'll be here shortly. What room does he have?"

Yoshi checked the reservation list. Then she ran her finger down it a second time before she looked up, frowning. "Did you say Colby? Is it spelled the way it sounds?"

"I suppose so." Cristina's brows drew together. "The first name is Webb. He said he had a confirmation letter."

The Japanese girl painstakingly went down the list one more time. "I can't find any Colby. Perhaps he made the reservation under another name."

"It's possible. He didn't mention it, though. I suppose we'll find out when he gets here. If he was leading me on all the time . . ."

"How do you mean—leading you on?"

A vision of Tessa's nose happily poking through the station wagon window as the car had disappeared up the drive flashed in Cris's mind, but all she said was, "Mr. Colby looked like the difficult type. You know what I mean—one of those men who hasn't taken 'no' for an answer in years."

"Old and crochety?" Yoshi asked, scenting some excitement.

"Not old," Cris said, after a barely perceptible pause, "but very decided."

"How old?"

"Thirty or thereabouts. I didn't ask him," Cristina said lightly.

"Good-looking?"

"I suppose you could say so. For heaven's sake, what difference does it make?"

Yoshi giggled and reached for the reservation list again. "If he's that attractive, I'll make sure we have a vacant room. Who cares about a reservation?"

"I do." Cristina tried to sound like a proper assistant manager and then spoiled it by adding, "Imagine what Kazy would say if he heard you!"

"He'd say it was about time someone interesting checked into this place. I know that we need the tour groups, but it would be nice if they included some eligible men under forty once in a while. It would certainly improve the scenery."

"Most people come here to look at another kind of scenery."

"I believe in variety myself." Yoshi's black eyes twinkled. "You don't sound as if you were completely immune to the idea either."

Cris smiled back at her. "There's no hope for you. Wait until you see the man. He isn't our type of guest at all."

"If he still has his own teeth—he isn't. Aside from that, what do you mean?"

"I'll bet my next week's salary that the only hiking he's done has been between a swimming pool and a tennis court on a Palm Springs guest ranch."

"Sounds better and better. Let's call Kazy in to take some lessons," Yoshi said flippantly. Then she sobered as she surveyed the list of names again. "Seriously, are you going to make room for Mr. Colby?"

Cristina couldn't very well admit that Mr. Colby's Irish setter was her primary concern. She merely said, "Yes, we might as well. We have those two rooms in the annex to handle overflow."

Yoshi looked doubtful. "It's a long walk."

"That shouldn't bother him," Cris said, well aware that the rooms were not convenient to the lobby but they were providently close to the fire escape stairs.

"Whatever you say." Yoshi lowered her voice as she heard the telltale squeak of the door to the manager's office. William Brock had given repeated orders to have the hinges oiled—and even stood over the maintenance man when it was done—but somehow the piercing squeak remained. Only Cris suspected that the staff on the reception desk made sure that their early-warning system remained intact.

"Ah . . . Cristina. You are just the person I want to see," Brock said as he strode out of his office with a letter clutched in his hand. He was a partially bald man in his late fifties, dressed in gray tweed sport coat and charcoal trousers His lodge guests appeared in every conceivable type of hiking gear and informal leisure outfit, but the only time Cristina had ever seen the manager out of his coat and tie was when he replaced them with a dressier outfit for the nighttime social events.

Since guests at the lodge only encountered the

buoyant side of his nature, there was no reason for complaint. And if the manager had needed further testimonial, he only had to point out that the lodge balance sheet finally was showing black ink.

That morning, however, his thin lips were clamped together more tightly than usual as he demanded the reservation list.

Yoshi handed it to him and watched his stubby finger go down the list of names before she said hastily, "If it's about Mr. Colby—Miss Kelly and I have just arranged to put him in an overflow room in the annex."

"Colby?" Brock's gaze came up again. "Who's talking about a Colby? I'm looking for the Schafers. Two couples from Santa Barbara who are due to arrive today. They phoned a few minutes ago from Portland." He slapped the register down on the counter in front of the Japanese girl. "Since they didn't receive the usual confirmation, they're a little upset. And since I don't see their names on the list," he continued, his voice rising sarcastically, "they're not the only ones. Now you tell me that there's some other trouble besides. Colby, was it?"

"Anything wrong?" came a quiet query from behind Cris.

She was so intent on the scene in front of her that she jumped a full three inches. "Oh, it's you. Mr. Brock—this is Mr. Colby, the guest we were discussing." She kept her gaze steadfastly on Webb's left ear as she continued, "There seems to have been a mixup with your reservation. We couldn't find your name on the list, but there's a single room in the annex with a view of the mountain, if that's all right." She felt a moment of triumph when she caught the manager's annoyed grimace. If he'd had a chance, Webb would have been sent firmly on his way. And if he ever learned about Tessa, Cristina thought gloomily, she'd be sharing the doghouse as well.

"The annex will be fine," Webb announced promptly, showing he was aware of the overtones.

Brock didn't give up easily. "We'll have to find room for the Schafer party first since it's a prior commitment. Naturally I'm sorry if we've inconvenienced you, Mr. Colby, but a reservation is paramount in this busy season. Ordinarily, we'd make exceptions—" A puzzled look came over his face as he saw Webb pull a letter from his pocket. "What's that?" Brock asked uneasily.

"My confirmed reservation," Webb replied. "I was out of the country at the time, so a friend made it for me."

Yoshi's pale cheeks took on added color as she peered at the letter and then at the well-thumbed register. "It was listed under your friend's name by mistake, Mr. Colby. I'm very sorry."

"No problem." Webb turned to the gray-haired man beside her. "Isn't that right, Mr. Brock?"

"Er, yes—of course. Except that you've requested one of our more deluxe rooms." Brock turned irritably to Cris. "The annex room isn't what we promised. That isn't our policy, Miss Kelly."

"It doesn't matter in the least," Webb said before she was forced to explain. "The annex will do very well. Now—if I can register and be shown to my room . . ."

Brock only had time to say, "This young lady will take care of that," before Yoshi slid a card across the counter and handed a pen to Webb. The manager settled his tie firmly in his collar as the crisis evaporated and sounded almost jovial as he added, "A boy will carry your luggage, Mr. Colby. Who's on duty, Cristina?"

"Jimmy." She looked over to the bell captain's bailiwick and could have groaned when she saw the empty desk. "He was here a minute ago." She tried to appear unconcerned. "If you'll wait a moment, Mr. Colby, I'll find him for you."

"There's no need. I can manage without any trouble," Webb said, giving the registration card to Yoshi. "If you'll just lead the way, Miss Kelly . . ."

"That won't be necessary—" Brock began angrily and broke off as Tom Warden came around the corner. "Mr. Warden will be glad to help you. Will you show Mr. Colby his room in the annex, Tom?"

The accountant took in the confusion at a glance as Webb straightened with his sleeping bag in one hand. Then Tom hastily stretched out his hand. "I thought I recognized you earlier. You probably don't remember me, Mr. Colby. We met at our head office in San Francisco last January. Warden's my name. Tom Warden. I'm the accountant here."

Cristina thought she saw a glimmer of irritation in Webb's face, but noticed that he concealed it immediately as he shook Tom's hand. "Nice of you to remember."

"I don't understand . . ." William Brock began. "I attended that meeting, too."

"But I didn't," Webb finished for him. "Mr. Warden will tell you that I simply escorted my mother to the office and left her there. It concerned her business, not mine."

Brock's color rose as facts registered. "Are you saying that Mrs. Regina Mathews is your mother?"

"That's right." If Webb was aware of Cristina's sudden indrawn breath, he didn't let on. Neither did he display any apparent interest in the man-

ager's ruddy complexion. He turned to Tom and
gestured toward the leather suitcase. "If you
wouldn't mind bringing that along, I'll carry the
rest."

Tom still hesitated as Brock took the room key
and surveyed it with some embarrassment. "I'm
sorry about not having better accommodation to
offer you right now, Mr. Colby," the older man
said, doing his best to recover lost ground.
"Naturally, your mother will be pleased to hear
that our business is so good."

Cristina's voice was tight as she cut into the
awkward pause which followed the manager's
words. "Probably you'd be more comfortable in the
chalet where I live, Mr. Colby. It's only fitting,
since Mrs. Mathews is part-owner of it." She went
on crisply, before he could interrupt, "I'm sure
you'll understand my reluctance to share the premises, but I'll be happy to move into the annex while
you're here."

Webb let his glance run over her stormy features. Finally he said in a flat voice, "I'll forget
about that damned silly suggestion if you will,
Miss Kelly," before taking the room key from
Brock's flaccid grasp and striding down the corridor.

Tom let his eyebrows climb as if to say "I
warned you" and then hastily picked up Colby's
case and hurried after him.

Chapter Two

* *

"Wow! What an exit line," Yoshi said as she watched them go. She turned to Cristina, forgetting momentarily about the manager at her elbow. "If that's how they do things in Palm Springs, I'm taking Kazy south for lessons this winter."

Her remark prompted William Brock to make one of his own. "If that young man of yours takes any lessons, I'd suggest something more in keeping with his work. Yesterday he spread three bales of bark in that flower bed by the bus parking area."

"What's wrong with that?" Yoshi asked in bewilderment.

"He completely covered the winter pansies that had been planted there the day before." The manager handed her the reservation list. "Double-check the dates on this for the rest of the month. I'd hate to learn of any more mistakes."

"I'll do it right away, Mr. Brock." She acknowledged Cristina's sympathetic glance with a grimace and headed toward a small room next to the manager's office.

Brock waited until the door had closed behind her before he pulled off his rimless glasses and squinted as he held them up to the light. Then he reached in his pocket for an immaculate handkerchief and started cleaning the lenses. "I gathered that you didn't know anything about Colby's plan to stay with us, Cristina."

She wasn't fooled by his casual tone. He was obviously upset; it showed in the way his fingers trembled as he put away his handkerchief and in the rigid line of his jaw.

"If I *had* known, I certainly wouldn't have been hanging over the kitchen porch ordering him to move his station wagon a little while ago," she said ruefully. "After that, I practically accused him of trying to get a room without a reservation, and then I told him . . ." Just in time she remembered about Tessa, who was probably still waiting in the hot car.

"You told him what?" Brock put his glasses back on and peered intently at her.

"I can't remember, but I'm sure it wasn't anything good." She chewed on her lower lip pensively. "I knew Mrs. Mathews inherited Lincoln Murray's interest in the lodge, and I think I even met her years ago—but no one ever mentioned a son. And why is his name Colby?"

Brock made an impatient sound. "There's no mystery about it. Her first husband was a man named Colby who died shortly after the boy was born. She married Leland Mathews a few years later. It was long before you had any interest in such things." Brock still sounded perturbed. "It's strange Mrs. Mathews didn't send a message to me so we could prepare for Colby's arrival. She's a very pleasant woman—not the type to do anything furtive or underhanded."

"Oh, for heaven's sakes!" Cristina was torn between irritation and laughter. "Nothing's happened to get all excited about. Probably her son found himself in this part of the country and just wanted a decent place to stay."

"That may be," Brock persisted stubbornly, "but I'm still surprised Mrs. Mathews didn't at least let *you* know about it, if not me."

Cris made no effort to hide her amusement then. "How old would you say he was?"

"Colby? I don't know. Thirty-two, thirty-three—somewhere around there."

"Exactly. Hardly the age for his mother to pin a note on his shirt pocket. If he's a typical man," she added wryly, "he probably didn't even tell her he was going to be here."

"I never thought of that." Brock frowned as he considered it, and then nodded. "You could be right. However, now that we know who he is, we certainly can't abandon him in a single room in the annex. At least I can't," he added more explicitly.

Cris could see the manager's point. An owner's son, no matter how unexpected his arrival, couldn't be left to languish in odd corners.

"What do you suggest?" She tried to sound as if she cared. "A special dinner? Or how about roping him into the next party climbing Rainier. That would take care of him for the entire weekend. Maybe longer."

"That's a very bad pun, Cristina. You're either short of sleep or sickening for something. I hope you're not going to be under the weather now that we're so busy."

"I'm fine." She looked around for her coffee, feeling by then that she needed a second cup. "Or at least I was when I got up this morning."

Brock's glance lit on the abandoned mug. "You could go and see if Colby's settled and then invite him for coffee. It would be a good way to tell him about the activities we have to offer."

"They're listed in the brochure in his room."

"I'm aware of that."

Cristina didn't need a brochure to understand the silence which fell between them. "All right. I'll stop by and see if there's anything he'd like."

"Good. And after that, try to think of something special that we can plan in his honor. I'd like him to go back to San Francisco full of enthusiasm about the way things are going here. I know we've had difficulties in past months at the lodge, but there's certainly nothing for Mrs. Mathews to criticize now." He looked at his watch. "It's time I checked the kitchen—I'll see you later."

Cristina set off herself, noting the still-empty bellman's desk as she made her way through the deserted lobby. Probably Jimmy had doubled back to the kitchen and was now on his third cup of coffee. It would serve the rascal right if Mr. Brock caught him in the middle of it.

That uncharitable thought carried her out into the sunshine and around toward the side door to the annex. There was activity far down at the end of the parking lot, where a steady stream of recreational vehicles was pulling in to disgorge a new day's crop of hikers. The rest of the parked cars belonged to lodge guests, and Cris took a shortcut past them as she headed toward the drive.

She saw Webb's station wagon a few minutes later, pulled up by the end of the annex. As she drew alongside, she was relieved to see that the dog had been removed, together with the rest of Webb's possessions. She hurried on up the steps of the building and used her passkey to open the metal fire door, wondering whether Webb already had Tessa in his room or was trying to camouflage her in the thick stand of trees beyond the parked cars.

As she stepped inside, she ran a professional glance along the hall corridor. It was light and cheerful, with golden yellow carpeting blending pleasantly with a paler yellow color on the walls. Guest-room doors were of natural pecan paneling trimmed with brass hardware.

Nothing for Webb to find fault with there, Cris decided, and then frowned a moment later when there was no answer to her knock on the door of his room. A second rapping brought the same result, and she found herself wondering if Tom had delivered the man to the wrong floor.

Automatically, she used her master key and opened the door. She had just taken a hesitant step into the room when she heard someone behind her.

"I didn't expect company so soon." Webb's deep voice held just enough disdain to make Cris's face turn pink. "Informality is the keynote in all lodge activities . . ." He quoted the resort's publicity brochure as he leaned against the threshold. "Tell me, Miss Kelly, how informal do you get here? I didn't hope to find you waiting for me in my room."

"Don't be ridiculous. I didn't think you were here." she managed to say. "I mean . . . I simply wondered if you'd been shown to the right room. Tom doesn't usually act as a bellman on the side."

"So he told me." Webb said casually. He reached behind him to close the door and gestured her toward the only upholstered piece in the room, a small chintz-covered chair in front of the window. "Since you're here, won't you sit down."

The words were courteous enough, but Webb's tone held little enthusiasm. Cristina flashed him an annoyed glance which showed that she recognized the deficiency as she stayed stubbornly on her feet. "That isn't necessary. I just came along to see if the dog was all right. What have you done with her?"

"Tessa? She's on her way home. I met the hiking party when I was driving through the parking lot. Charles was happy to reclaim his property."

Cristina frowned. "Charles—oh, you mean your friend."

"That's right. He lives up this way. The dog had to be left in a kennel while he was out on the trail. Naturally he wanted to retrieve her as soon as possible." Webb smiled wryly. "I hadn't realized that Tessa was going to cause such a furor when I arrived."

"I'm sorry about that . . ."

He shrugged. "Rules are rules. No one blames you."

"Of course, if you'd said who you were, the rules could have been bent," she added pointedly.

"I thought we'd get around to that sooner or later. Sit down, Miss Kelly . . ."

This time there was nothing of an invitation in his words. It was a terse order, and Cristina reacted automatically, sinking into the chair before she even thought about it.

Webb walked over to perch on the end of the small walnut desk. "I don't see why my appearance caused such a commotion. My mother's talked about the lodge for years, and when I found that I'd have some spare time in the northwest, I simply decided to spend a few days here."

Cris stared at him. He'd abandoned his blazer, but other than that, loosening his tie had been his only concession to the surroundings. Probably he was the only man in the lodge other than the manager who could be found in a white shirt at that hour of the morning. She smothered her amusement as she said, "Of course, Mr. Colby. I hope you enjoy your stay with us. You'll find things a little quieter here than at the usual resort. Most of our guests come for the scenery or the hiking" She eyed his immaculately pressed trousers. "We could find a guide for you, and I'm sure Tom Warden could help outfit you if you'd like to try some of the trails," she added helpfully.

There was an instant's pause while the man lounging against the desk stared at her. "That's kind of you," he said finally. "Warden looked about my size, so maybe I could borrow some gear. I suppose I'd need a different kind of shirt . . ."

"And shoes and pants," Cris told him briskly. "The trails around here are well-tended, but they have a marked degree of difficulty. I'd suggest you start on something close to the lodge."

"That sounds sensible." Webb got up to stare out the window at the snow-covered outlines of the mountain. "I'm impressed by your scenery already."

Cris felt a pricking of guilt and wondered if she had been too impulsive in condemning him. It wasn't his fault that he was simply out of his element. "There's nothing that can compete with our mountain," she said in a more kindly tone. "I've lived in this part of the United States most of my life and I still get a thrill each time I see Rainier." When he didn't reply but continued to stare through the window, she gathered her courage to probe further. "Mr. Colby, did your mother tell you anything about the problems we've had here at the lodge?"

"What kind of problems?" he asked, turning to face her.

"Well, actually nothing lately. There were some things that happened before I arrived. Just about the time my grandfather first became ill."

"We were sorry to hear about his death," Webb said quietly. "I only met him once, but my mother admired him greatly." He came back to sit on the edge of the desk again. "Exactly what are you doing here, Miss Kelly? Are you planning a life's work in the resort business?"

"Nothing like that. I have a perfect right to work here, Mr. Colby. If you want to stick around and represent your mother's interests, Mr. Brock will find something for you to do as well." Her glance swept over him disdainfully, letting him know that it wouldn't be easy to find anything in his line.

"God forbid! This isn't my scene at all," Webb said immediately, letting her know that she didn't have to worry on that score.

"I didn't imagine it was," she replied sweetly. "Well, we'll do our best to make your brief stay enjoyable," she added, getting up and starting for the door. "Mr. Brock and I will be on duty all day."

"Just a minute." His voice caught her before she'd taken more than a few steps. "You said something about earlier problems here at the lodge."

"They're past now. I don't know why I brought them up."

"My mother might think differently," he pointed out.

"I'm sure she read about them in the management reports. There was no attempt to hide anything."

"That may be," he confirmed. "Except I was

away at that time and now you've whetted my curiosity."

Cristina gave him a level look. "Do you ever take 'no' for an answer, Mr. Colby?"

"Practically never. Will you sit down again."

"No, thanks, it isn't necessary." She took a deep breath, wondering how his masculine presence seemed to take up every bit of space in the room. "We didn't advertise our difficulties here at the lodge, but we had a hard time weathering the storm. Not literally," she admitted with a wry smile. "That was one trouble. The winter season was balmy, with sunshine, clear days, and practically no snow for our skiers. That would have been bad enough in itself . . ."

"But there was more?"

"Oh, yes." Her voice took on a bitter edge. "One weekend, we suffered a rash of broken pipes—and the plumbing bill afterward resembled the national debt. Two weeks later, someone started a rumor about food poisoning from our kitchen. By the time the health inspectors cleared us of the charges, our reservation list had so many holes in it that it could have doubled as a pincushion. About that time my grandfather became ill and"—she steadied her voice with an effort—"I came back to help."

"You must have worked the miracle." Webb walked to the window and turned his back, giving her time to collect herself. "Things look prosperous here at the lodge now."

"For the moment. Mr. Brock and I still have our fingers crossed, though."

"It sounds as if you're due for some good luck, if the plumbing and the food fiascos were just part of doing business."

Her glance met his in some surprise. "There was

no evidence that they weren't. Naturally the management company officials questioned Mr. Brock at the time. They weren't happy about the financial statement they had to present that quarter."

"I can understand that." Webb rattled some change in his pocket as he thought for a minute. Then he asked, "Who was the beneficiary of your grandfather's estate?"

His question was so abrupt that Cris found herself answering involuntarily. "It went into a trust, Mr. Colby." Her lips tightened as she added, "I can see why your mother might be interested, but other than that . . ." The words trailed off significantly.

"It's no concern of mine," he finished for her. "You're right. I won't keep you any longer." He opened the door while she was still reaching for it. "Thank you for your efforts on Tessa's behalf. You'll have to meet her owner. He'll be stopping by again while I'm here."

Cris managed to nod and felt like a long-distance runner at the finish line when the door closed behind her.

The rest of the morning passed uneventfully. Cristina divided her time between checking rooms with the housekeeper, arranging the extra produce delivery, and going over food costs with the dining room manager. At noon, she walked back to the chalet to make a quick sandwich and found herself strangely disappointed when she didn't catch a glimpse of Webb Colby either coming or going.

William Brock finally satisfied her curiosity about him late in the afternoon when Cristina was watching a tour-bus guide rounding up passengers in the lobby. "There's no use planning anything special for Colby tonight," the manager announced, emerging from his office and walking over to her.

"I hadn't given it a thought," she replied, not quite truthfully. "What's the matter? Was the great outdoors too much for him today?"

"I don't know. I didn't ask. Didn't have a chance, as a matter of fact. He left a message with the telephone operator that he wasn't to be disturbed until late afternoon. After that, he made a dinner reservation for two. Must be expecting company."

"Probably Tessa's owner," Cris murmured without thinking.

Brock's eyebrows drew together. "That sounds very strange."

"Not when you know that Tessa's a red setter," Cristina said. "You've been a hotel manager too long."

"Today I'll agree with you. I had words with that bellboy when he reappeared this morning." Brock nodded genially to an elderly guest and waited for the old gentleman to get out of hearing before going on. "I told the young man that since he found the early morning shift such a chore after his social activities, he could switch to night duty for the rest of the week."

Cristina nodded and brought the subject back to the topic uppermost in her mind. "It doesn't sound as if Mr. Colby needs any help with his social schedule."

"Well, it won't hurt to ask," Brock said, automatically straightening a pen holder on the reception desk. "I doubt if he knows many people around here."

"Not if he spent the day sleeping. I don't know why we bothered to give him a view of the moun-

tain," she said disdainfully. "He probably kept the
curtains pulled the entire time."

"There could be a perfectly plausible excuse.
Maybe the altitude bothers him. He'll soon feel
better, once he's gotten accustomed to it."

Just then, Cristina caught sight of a tall familiar
figure, and she turned her back so Webb wouldn't
suspect that he was the subject under discussion.
"From the way he looks, he isn't suffering very
much," she confided to Brock in an undertone.

"You mean he's around?" The older man spun
around eagerly, and only the fact that Webb was
disappearing into the gift shop to buy a newspaper
kept the manager from scuttling over to greet him
then and there.

"I'll be going," Cris said hastily, intent on getting
away before Brock could waylay the other. "See
you in the morning."

"All right." Brock nodded absently and then surprised Cristina with a soft whistle which made her
turn back again. "What is it?" she started to ask before she followed his intent glance.

A newspaper wasn't the only thing Webb Colby
had collected at the gift shop. At that moment, he
was unhurriedly extricating himself from an embrace with one of the most striking blondes that
Cristina had ever seen. The young woman, in a
snug-fitting navy and white suit of couturier
design, looked like a Scandinavian model en route
to Hollywood. Her pale hair was long and straight,
combed back just enough to reveal high Nordic
cheekbones and a superb complexion. She was
taller than average but beautifully proportioned,
and it was easy to see why Webb was slow about
lowering his arms.

By that time, the two of them had a considerable

audience. It was unfortunate that Cristina's glance was the first one that Webb intercepted as he turned toward the cocktail lounge.

Cris hurriedly dropped her gaze but not before she'd seen an amused flicker pass over his face and watched him change his route deliberately.

"I'm glad you're both still on duty," he said, keeping the blonde close beside him as they pulled up in front of the reception desk. "I'd like to present Mrs. Simmons—an old friend of mine. Sheila, this is Miss Kelly and Mr. Brock." He smiled down at his "old" friend as he went on to explain, "Miss Kelly assists Mr. Brock, who's the very efficient manager here."

William Brock said, "Delighted to know you, Mrs. Simmons," in response to Sheila Simmons' dazzling smile. His tone was so different from normal that Cris shot him an incredulous look before she managed a polite "How do you do" of her own.

"How I envy you both," Sheila said, revealing a soft voice as delightful as her profile. "This is the loveliest place—I've always wanted to stay here. But now that I've arrived, Webb says there isn't a room to be had. Is that right?" Her blue eyes fixed beseechingly on the older man.

Brock ran a finger around his collar. "Unfortunately, it's absolutely true, Mrs. Simmons. Of course, if Mr. Colby had just given us a little notice, we could have made other arrangements." He let his voice drop regretfully.

Sheila Simmons turned to Cristina for another try. "Not even a broom closet? Honestly, I'd be glad for anything."

"I'm sorry, but Mr. Brock's right," Cristina said. She met Webb's stare without flinching. "There's another resort called The Crescent about ten miles down the road. If you like, I'll call and see if they have any rooms tonight."

Webb couldn't very well quarrel with her courteous manner. Only the tightening of his lips showed that he wasn't exactly pleased. "I suppose that might be the best solution. It'll be more convenient if you stay in the neighborhood until there's something at the lodge, Sheila," he said, reassuring the woman at his side.

William Brock hurriedly seconded Webb's decision. "Miss Kelly can call The Crescent right away, Mrs. Simmons. We'll send word to you in the bar if that's where you two are headed. And naturally we'll see that you have the first room that becomes available here. Isn't that right, Cristina?"

"I'll make a note of it." She managed a pleasant smile as she said, "If you'll excuse me, I'll call The Crescent now. It was nice meeting you, Mrs. Simmons."

"Just a minute." Webb stopped her before she could escape. "If you have trouble reaching The Crescent right away, we'll be in the dining room a little later."

"Don't worry, Cristina will find you. She's absolutely reliable," Brock assured him.

"The epitome of virtue, eh?" Webb's glance showed amusement as it flicked over Cristina. "I must tell my mother how fortunate she is."

Sheila put a hand on his wrist. "I may have a few things to tell her myself by then. Now let's hurry, or there won't be time for a drink before dinner."

"Coming—right away." He nodded impersonally to Brock and Cristina and led Mrs. Simmons toward the cocktail lounge with its rustic entrance.

Brock's expression wasn't quite as bemused as

before. "Did you catch that remark about Mrs. Mathews?"

"Loud and clear," Cris said. "I got the impression that Mrs. Simmons isn't used to not finding room at the inn. Don't worry," she added reassuringly. "Mr. Colby didn't miss that remark either. I don't think you have to worry about Mrs. Mathews getting the wrong idea." She caught up a pencil and note pad.

Brock followed her back to her desk and telephone. "He doesn't appear to miss much of anything. I was surprised at that 'epitome of virtue' comment, though. What did you say to him earlier?"

"Apparently not enough." Cristina picked up the receiver and smiled tightly. "Sometime this weekend I guess I'll have to map a hike for Mr. Colby and his charming lady friend. It would be nice for them to have something special to remember, don't you think?"

Brock put his hand to his forehead. "I didn't hear that. And if anything goes wrong while he's here . . ."

"What could go wrong?" She cut in, wide-eyed with innocence.

The older man made an unidentifiable sound in his throat. "Only two more years until retirement and I'm getting caught in the crossfire now! How could I be so lucky?"

"You mean—two major stockholders in residence." She frowned slightly and hesitated before saying, "There's no need to mention that in front of Mr. Colby. He knows that my grandfather brought me back to work here. I'd rather leave it at that."

"Keep him in the dark, eh?" Brock's expression was thoughtful as he considered her heightened color. "I wondered why he didn't say anything about your interests when he introduced you to his girl friend."

"Well, that's why. She wouldn't have been enchanted with the news. I'll call down and ask The Crescent for an overflow room." Cristina picked up the telephone receiver and grinned wickedly. "How long should we keep Mrs. Simmons in suspense about a roof over her head?"

"That's up to you. As of now, I'm off-duty. You can handle any repercussions."

"Not this time." Her grin was unrepentant. "I'm off-duty, too. Tom's around somewhere—he can notify Mrs. Simmons. He has a fondness for blondes."

"From the way he talks, he's more impressed with getting to know Colby while he's here. This lodge isn't close enough to headquarters as far as Tom's career is concerned." He shook his head. "Although why anybody would choose the hotel business when he could settle down in a nice peaceful accounting firm is beyond me."

"Because of the fascinating people we meet. That's what you told me the first day I came to work here."

"Well, I've had my quota of fascination for today. If anyone wants me, I'll be in my quarters. Are all the shifts covered?"

"I'll double-check before I leave." Her attention switched as her phone call came through. "Hello . . . Crescent . . . This is Cris Kelly. Will you connect me with reception, please?"

"See you tomorrow," Brock mouthed.

She nodded, waving a casual farewell, and settled down to finding accommodation for Webb's glamorous girl friend.

A little later, she tracked Tom Warden down in

the soda fountain and grinned as she pushed his coffee mug out of reach. "You're wasting your time in here, my friend. All the action's in the bar tonight." She waved a memo sheet in front of his puzzled face. "This is your introduction to the most gorgeous blonde who's entered these premises since that cabaret singer showed up in June."

He brightened as he thought about it. "The one who claimed she'd been hired by the bartender for after-dinner entertainment?"

"I thought you'd remember."

He nodded, grinning. "It was a damned shame she couldn't carry a tune."

"Exactly what you said at the time. Along with Mr. Brock and every other assorted male within sight."

Tom's smile widened. "Don't tell me she has a sister."

"You'll have to ask the bartender about that." Cris tucked the memo into his fingers. "In the meantime, you've won the lucky dip for tonight. Take that into the bar and look for a beautiful blonde sitting next to our Mr. Colby. All you have to do is introduce yourself and say that we have confirmed her reservation for tonight at The Crescent."

"The Crescent!" Tom's yelp of surprise so startled the girl behind the counter that the soft ice cream sundae she was concocting came perilously close to disaster.

Cristina gave her an apologetic grimace and tugged Tom toward the lobby before anything worse happened.

"If the blonde is that much of a dish and a friend of Colby's, why in the devil are you sending her down the road to The Crescent," Tom wanted to know, lingering stubbornly by the fountain door.

"Because we don't have any place for her to sleep here unless you're offering the top of your desk."

"I'll pitch a tent on it if it will help my cause at the main office. Do you suppose Webb Colby has anything to do with personnel promotions?" he asked hopefully.

"I doubt if he'd recognize one end of a paycheck from the other," Cris said. "Chances are he's only familiar with remittance checks from his mother."

Tom's expression was skeptical. "I think you've pegged him wrong . . ."

"Maybe—but he's not the typical lodge guest. Tonight he'll be the only man in the bar who isn't wearing a sport shirt."

"That will endear him to Brock. He's always bemoaning the informality around here."

"Probably because most hikers leave their vests and stuffed shirts at home." Then she added ruefully, "Actually it's sour grapes on my part. Mrs. Simmons is wearing an elegant outfit. She certainly rates more than jeans and boots from an escort."

Tom ignored the last part of her sentence. "Did you say *Mrs.* Simmons? Damn! I thought she was available." He frowned down at Cris. "Is there a Mr. Simmons?"

She moved the memo to his pocket and said, "If you don't take that in pretty soon, there won't even be a Mrs. Simmons on the premises."

"If there were a husband around," Tom theorized, "Webb Colby wouldn't have invited her for the weekend."

Cris was inclined to agree with him, but the logic of his argument didn't improve her disposition. "Maybe he has a different set of rules," she snapped. "I'm leaving now—good luck on your prowl."

"For pete's sake, what's the matter with you?"

"Not a thing," she lied. "It's just been one of those days. I'll see you tomorrow."

Tom nodded and turned toward the bar, already intent on a chance to improve his acquaintance with the owner's son and meet an attractive woman at the same time.

Cristina felt an instant's chagrin. Until then, Tom had remained loyally by her side at the lodge's social events, although their relationship had stayed easy and informal. Now abruptly his attention was starting to waver.

She shook her head and walked out of the lodge. When she reached the flagstone terrace, she stopped for a moment to enjoy the last rays of the sunset painting the mountain's icy sides with a glorious pinkish-orange glow. The lower peaks of the Tatoosh range were sharply outlined against the sky, their tree-covered slopes resembling precise silhouette cutouts on a giant work of art.

She smiled, never failing to feel impressed by the presence of the rugged scenery around her. It wasn't strange; the early Indians had held the mountain's pinnacles in awe and had only hunted the lower slopes of Tahoma, as they called it, avoiding the dangers of the higher elevations. Modern hikers and climbers accorded the peak the same respect—only the name was changed, Cristina mused as she walked toward her chalet. In 1792, Captain George Vancouver had called the mountain Rainier in honor of his friendship with Peter Rainier. The British rear admiral never saw his namesake, and some local residents were still inclined to resent the change.

Her thoughts were suddenly interrupted by a shout of "Hey, Cris!" and she turned to see Yoshi and Kazy waving from the edge of the parking lot.

She waved back and called, "How was your afternoon?"

"Great! The trail could use some repairs though." Kazy lifted an obviously empty picnic basket. "Thanks for arranging the lunch. We needed it—Yoshi can't cook."

"Don't pay any attention to him," Yoshi cut in. "Did everything go all right this afternoon at the lodge? Mr. Brock didn't mind?"

"Everything's okay," Cris reassured her. "Leave him a note about the maintenance needed in that section of trail and everybody will love you. See you in the morning."

A few minutes later she closed the door of the chalet behind her and pulled the long drapes at the living room windows. She stood by the curtains, savoring the refuge the comfortable room provided. Then, on an impulse, she went over and lit a fire in the big native-stone fireplace to her right. Ridiculous to want a fireplace fire in August, she told herself, even as she sank down on one of the brown leather chairs in front of it. She let her gaze go over the cinnamon carpet and the honey shades of birch paneling on the walls. There were brass reading lamps beside the upholstered pieces and hidden ceiling lighting to make the kitchen corner with its copper-colored appliances bright and cheerful on even the darkest winter day. A short hallway led to a guest bedroom and bathroom behind the living area downstairs, but a wrought-iron spiral staircase provided access to the balcony loft which Cristina had adopted for her bedroom and dressing area.

After all that had happened, she harbored an inexplicable urge to climb those stairs and collapse on the bed, pulling the covers over her head. She'd left the lodge feeling as if she'd spent hours in a giant cement mixer and had just been spilled out on the ground.

Which was absurd, she told herself firmly. It was true that the day had been hectic, but there'd been worse days since she'd come back. Of course, on other days she hadn't had to contend with Webb Colby, as well. Nor any blonde *enamorada*.

Even that fleeting thought of Sheila Simmons was enough to make Cris get abruptly to her feet and head for the stairway to change her clothes. She couldn't sit around mooning all night—she'd fix dinner for herself and put on a favorite record. For a moment, she even wished that television reception was possible in the mountains because it was so helpful in reducing one's thinking processes to jelly.

She was sensible enough to realize that life would probably look much better in the morning, once she'd had dinner and a decent night's sleep. In addition, there was the niggling possibility that The Crescent wouldn't suit Sheila Simmons at all. The gorgeous blonde might disappear down the road in search of more civilized trappings after a brief one-night stand in the neighborhood.

Cristina was surprised to discover how much satisfaction that particular thought gave her.

Chapter Three

❖❖❖❖❖❖❖❖❖❖❖❖❖❖❖❖❖❖❖❖❖❖❖❖❖❖❖

It wasn't the usual clamor of her alarm clock on the bed table which awoke her in the early hours of the morning, but the sound of the big brass fire bell on the lodge annex.

Cris sat bolt upright, her heart pounding in her ears so loudly that it almost drowned out the bell's tolling. For an instant she remained immobile—sure that the commotion outside was all part of a nightmare rather than reality. Then she came to life and scrambled into her clothes with a speed that rivaled a fireman's. She was pulling on a sweater as she raced down the stairs and tore across the living room to the front door. Inwardly she was braced for the sight of flames licking the sides of the lodge, and she felt a relief so intense that it almost left her gasping when she opened the door and found the huge building outwardly unchanged except for excited clusters of people streaming out the fire exits.

The guests were in every sort of attire, from women wearing chiffon negligees topped by down parkas to men clad only in jeans and pajama tops. Just then she was so happy to see them obviously unharmed and even laughing as they reached the ground that the outlandish outfits went almost unnoticed.

She didn't linger among them but hurried up the stairs at the end of the annex, threading her way past four stragglers who were just coming down. Even then she was hoping that someone had rung the fire bell by mistake. As soon as she pushed around the edge of the big metal door leading into the corridor she realized that it was no false alarm.

Sour, pungent billows of smoke hung in the hallway, making her eyes smart and start to water as she walked through the haze. She flattened against a wall as three more women hurried past, and then heard a fire marshal at the far end of the corridor sound "all clear," which meant that the last guest was out of the annex.

Just then, the door of a staff room ten feet down the hall opened and a crowd of people emerged, two still holding fire extinguishers and another carrying a metal wastebasket piled high with charred curtain remnants. Smoke eddied out into the hallway after them, but it thinned perceptibly even as she watched.

There were two people left in the staff bedroom when Cristina made her way to the threshold and peered anxiously in. Kazy was beside a smoke-blackened window wall, staring unhappily at still-dripping sprinklers on the ceiling and Webb Colby in dark slacks and a grimy turtleneck stood frowning nearby.

Cris had to clear her throat before she could speak. Then all she could finally manage was, "Is it out?"

Both men turned to stare at her as if she had sprouted another head. Webb recovered first, but Cristina could tell that he was controlling his irritation with difficulty as he said, "It damned well better be."

Kazy was more respectful. "Everything's okay now, Miss Kelly. Fortunately, the fire didn't get much of a start before the sprinklers were triggered. When Mr. Colby came in, only this wall was still ablaze and he took care of that." Kazy gestured toward a fire extinguisher on the floor.

Cris's expression mirrored her dismay as she turned toward the other man. "How did you get here so fast?"

"I didn't have far to come. My room's just down the hall, and I hadn't been in bed long when I smelled smoke." He absently rubbed his jaw and then frowned as he saw the soot on his hand.

"You must be more of a night owl than the rest of us."

"Not really. I had to make sure Sheila arrived at The Crescent in one piece." He surveyed the dripping mess of the room around him dispassionately. "From the looks of things, I would have been better off to stay down there, too."

Kazy nodded agreement. "It'll take a day or two before this room dries out, that's for sure."

"Who does it belong to?" Cristina wanted to know.

"Jimmy Bolton." Kazy gave out the information reluctantly.

"I might have known." Her glance was resigned as it swept the bare top of the chest of drawers and the desk. "Did he get his things out before they were damaged?"

"Somebody took care of it for him," Kazy muttered. "One of the fire marshals."

"Jimmy—Jimmy Bolton." Webb repeated the name thoughtfully. "That wouldn't be the elusive bellhop, would it?"

"The one and only," Cristina admitted. She

turned back to Kazy. "From the way you're tippy-toeing around the subject, I gather that Jimmy is among the missing again?"

"Not officially. He did mention he'd made a date down at The Crescent tonight that he couldn't cancel."

Cris shook her head as if to clear it. "Well, there'll be time to cope with that later. Right now, I'd better help get the guests back to their rooms. They'll have to put up with the smoke smell, but we can all be thankful that there's nothing worse. Has Mr. Brock been down?"

"Right in the thick of things," Webb said. "When he found events were under control here, he went out to evacuate the customers. You have a damned good system for getting people out of the building."

Kazy spoke up. "We work hard at it—don't we, Miss Kelly?"

"Absolutely—and you certainly get 'A' for effort tonight." She stood aside to let two of the clean-up crew come in with mops and buckets. "I'll be back later."

For the next hour, her job kept her in the lobby of the lodge. Even though it had been established that there was no further danger from the fire, most of the guests were reluctant to return to their rooms. The atmosphere of excitement turned festive, and their odd costumes added zest to the occasion. When the kitchen staff served coffee and sandwiches, someone turned on the record player and within minutes an impromptu party was born.

"As long as everybody's happy, we'd be foolish to try and break things up," William Brock said, coming over beside Cris as she poured coffee. "It looks like the best party we've had all season." He reached absently for a sandwich and started to munch on it.

Cris gave him an amused sideways glance. Evidently he had forgotten the impeccable appearance he set such store by. Just then, his gray hair was rumpled, and he was wearing a pair of trousers obviously slipped on hurriedly over his pajamas. His only concession to formality was an elegant green silk robe for the top layer.

"We'll have to include a 'Come as you are' dance in the schedule after this," Cris agreed, putting the coffeepot down finally when she ran out of customers. "It was an inspired idea of yours to serve food."

Brock's mouth twisted in an annoyed grimace. "I wish I could take credit for it—but I can't. Apparently Jimmy Bolton was down in the kitchen making himself a sandwich when the fire broke out. He took one look at the way things were going and decided to handle the catering end."

"So he finished with all the plaudits coming his way instead of the humble pie he deserved. Honestly, that boy!" Cris ran a weary hand over her forehead.

"He's not the only one who's put me in a difficult spot," Brock said, pouring himself a cup of coffee to go with the last bit of his sandwich.

When he didn't go on, Cris prompted him. "What do you mean?"

"It will take a full week to put those end rooms of the annex back in shape. The staff members have already agreed to double up, but obviously we can't ask Colby to get a sleeping bag and doss down here in the lobby."

A feeling of foreboding settled liked a rock in the middle of Cristina's stomach. She made herself take a deep breath before she said, "Go on—I'm listening."

"There's only one place fitting for him and that's your chalet," Brock said. "It's the only solution."

"You're right—I don't even have a legal leg to stand on. Mrs. Mathews owns half the place." She kept her tone easy. "Of course, there is another angle—we're fresh out of chaperones."

Brock's mouth took on a stubborn line. "Really, Cristina—I doubt if you have to worry about that. After meeting Mrs. Simmons here tonight, do you really think that Colby will infringe on your feminine—er—ah—hospitality?"

The suggestive way that he cleared his throat was enough to make Cris want to haul off and whack him with the empty sandwich tray by her hand. Then she realized that he was merely saying aloud what she knew all too well. Webb Colby wouldn't be looking for diversions when he had a gorgeous creature like Sheila Simmons just down the road. He'd already admitted that it had been well after midnight when he'd finally gotten around to taking her to The Crescent. Obviously they hadn't spent their time after dinner watching the color slide-show of northwest scenery which was scheduled in the lobby.

"Well, what's it going to be?" Brock was still watching her closely.

Cris felt a weariness settle over her that had nothing to do with the post-midnight goings-on. "He can have the guest room at the chalet." She reached over to absently brush some crumbs from the table and tossed them in the fireplace nearby. "Do I have to issue a formal invitation?"

"I doubt if he'd like to hear about it from young Jimmy." Brock waved genially to a couple of

guests who were forming a conga line on the other
side of the fireplace. "Idiots!" he complained for
Cris's ears alone. "I wish to hell they'd go to bed."

"I can stay around until they do . . ." she began.

"No, no, no." He put up an authoritative hand.
"This is my responsibility. You go find Colby and
make sure he's kept happy." He noted her startled
look and went on querulously, "Don't be difficult,
Cristina—not after everything that's happened
tonight."

"All right. I'm sorry." She smiled ruefully as she
looked at her watch. "I guess I'm not at my best at
three A.M."

"God, who is! Go collect Colby and find someone
to move his belongings. And once you get him
tucked away for the night, do your best to make
him sleep late tomorrow morning. I certainly intend to."

"Don't worry." She twirled an imaginary handle-
bar mustache and tried to approximate a vil-
lainous leer. "Once he's in my power—I'll lock the
door and throw away the key."

Brock managed a tired grin and waved her on
her way.

She found Webb still in the annex observing the
final mop-up of the smoke-damaged area. "We
missed you at the party in the lobby," she told him,
wishing she didn't sound quite so much like a professional social director.

The resemblance must have occurred to Webb
as well, but his expression didn't change as he said,
"The conga line got down here at one point so I
didn't miss all the festivities."

"That's good. I'm sorry you've been bothered
with all this." Cris could have told him that he
would have felt more at home if he'd joined the

party in the lobby. On the other hand, supervising the clean-up activity might help to impress his mother when he went back to California.

"I expected some inconvenience when I came," Webb drawled. He moved down the corridor to the open door of his room, where he hesitated on the threshold. "If there's nothing else . . ."

His obvious impatience to dispense with her company made Cris's cheeks go red with anger, and her determination to remain cool and polite went flying as she snapped, "Mr. Brock would rather you didn't stay here tonight. You certainly won't be comfortable sleeping in there." She jerked her head toward his quarters.

He studied her defiant figure for a moment. "And just where did Mr. Brock—and you—decide that I *would* be comfortable? Incidentally," he added before she could say anything, "don't suggest The Crescent. Their receptionist said that Sheila got their last room."

"I wasn't about to."

"That's a blessing." His tone matched hers for coldness. "Is Brock volunteering his office sofa?"

"He would if he had one. Unfortunately, there's only a small desk and a chair available."

Webb glanced at his watch deliberately. "Do you suppose we could play Twenty Questions some other time. Right now, I'd like to go back to bed." He looked over her shoulder to say in a friendlier tone, "Back again, Tom? I thought you'd given up for the night."

"I made the mistake of detouring by the lobby and Brock caught me." The accountant came up behind Cris and put a friendly arm over her shoulders. "He suggested that I help move Webb's stuff over to the chalet."

"Of course, what a good idea!" she said, trying to sound enthusiastic. "With three people, we only need to make one trip."

"Not even that," Webb spoke up finally. "I had Kazy put my stuff in the station wagon a little while ago. Most of it can be unloaded in the morning."

"Good! Then I can go to bed with a clear conscience," Tom said cheerfully. "Somebody will have to get some sleep around here if school keeps tomorrow. See you both in the morning." He gave Cris's shoulder an affectionate squeeze and nodded to Webb before disappearing back along the corridor.

There was an instant's silence after he'd left. Then Webb let his derisive glance rest on Cris. "The chalet, eh? No wonder you were stalling earlier."

"I don't know what you're talking about." She walked over to the fire exit at the end of the corridor. "You can drive across whenever you're ready. I'll go ahead and make your bed."

"Just a minute . . ." His voice caught her in midstep. "You're sure that this is all right with you, Cristina? After all, there's nothing in the fine print of your contract that says you have to harbor the enemy."

"Don't be absurd. I have a perfectly good guest room, and the least I can do is offer you a roof over your head. Expecially after you've worked so hard to save this roof tonight."

"But I had a selfish motive for that, didn't I?" He seemed to take a strange satisfaction in voicing the thoughts she'd been trying to ignore. "It was the least I could do to look after my family's interests and possibly a few of yours at the same time."

"I don't know why we have to get on that subject again," she reproved. "If you'll excuse me, I'll go on ahead."

"Such impeccable manners," he murmured with some amusement. "Even in the middle of the night."

Cristina realized that her dignified air was only as thick as a nail paring, and she chose to retreat rather than continue the verbal sparring. "I'll see you at the house," she managed over her shoulder and plunged down the fire stair as if flames were licking at her heels.

Fifteen minutes passed before Webb parked the station wagon at the side of the chalet, and Cristina had her composure firmly in hand when she greeted him at the front door. "You can take your things straight through to the bedroom. Just follow me," she instructed, and led the way through the living room to the small but well-furnished bedroom at the rear of the chalet. "The bathroom is right next door," she went on in the same bright impersonal tone, "and you can store your extra belongings in the utility room."

He was looking around the bedroom with an interested expression after depositing his bag on a rack under the window. "Very nice," he said, apparently approving the subdued rust and green color scheme before wandering on to poke his head in the bathroom.

"I've put your towels on the back of the door." Cristina tried to sound as if having a strange man as a house guest happened all the time. "Naturally, you'll probably prefer to go over to the dining room for your meals . . ."

"Naturally," he murmured, just as blandly.

". . . But feel free to help yourself in the kitchen."

"What do you do for food?" he asked, as he sent a lazy glance toward the copper-colored appliances and immaculate countertops.

Cristina was busily giving thanks that she'd done her dishes earlier that night and almost missed his question. "I beg your pardon?"

"Never mind." He walked out in the living room and surveyed the spiral stairway to the loft. "You sleep up there?"

"Why, yes." For a giddy moment, she thought he was going up to inspect the pattern of her sheets, and she let out an unconscious sigh of relief when he turned and strolled back toward the rear of the chalet. She was so unnerved by then that she blurted out, "What are you going to do?" without stopping to think.

Webb looked back at her. "I *was* going to bed. That was the general idea, wasn't it? Or did you have something else in mind?"

Pure unadulterated anger shot through her like a lightning bolt, and for a brief moment her fingers itched to slap his arrogant jaw—anything to wipe the laughter from those assured features. She tried to think of something frigid and scathing to say in reply and came up with the conversational gem of the evening—"Good night, Mr. Colby, I hope you sleep well"—before she turned and scuttled to the safety of the loft.

Chapter Four

❖❖❖❖❖❖❖❖❖❖❖❖❖❖❖❖❖❖❖❖❖❖❖

It was a combination of breakfast smells that finally awakened her the next morning.

She gave a pleased murmur and stretched luxuriously, thinking that nothing could top the fragrance of freshly brewed coffee and bacon frying in the pan. Then the events of the previous night came flooding back and she sat upright to stare around her in suspicion. Sun was streaming over the cheerful rag rug on the floor, and the air that came in the loft window felt as balmy as alpine air was ever inclined to be. The early morning tranquility of the chalet was apparently undisturbed; only the smell of food below revealed that Webb was up and stirring.

She slid over the edge of the mattress and felt with her toes for her slippers, bending down impatiently to look for them when they proved elusive. Then she remembered the speed with which she'd undressed the night before, a panicky maneuver which had precluded niceties like slippers and a robe. She probably wouldn't have managed pajamas if they hadn't been stored under her pillow.

Still barefooted, she padded over by the loft railing to peer at the deserted room below. Webb apparently had gone to the lodge after fixing his breakfast. Just as she reached that conclusion, one of the big glass panels opening onto the porch was abruptly shoved aside and he came back into the room, holding a pair of binoculars in his hand.

Her instinctive withdrawal caught his attention and his shoulders started to shake with laughter. Cristina was too stricken to retreat further although she knew how she must look in rumpled blue and white challis pajamas with her hair still uncombed. It didn't help that Webb was wearing sand-colored cotton slacks and a plaid cotton shirt that fitted as if it had been tailor-made.

She battened down an urge to get completely out of sight and leaned over the loft railing instead. "Good morning," she said. "I hope you slept well— all things considered."

"Fine, thanks," he replied, just as calmly, sliding the glass panel closed behind him. "There's coffee on the stove if you'd like some." The way he strolled over to sit in a leather chair and put his feet up on an ottoman showed that he had no intention of doing anything strenuous in the immediate future.

"Thank you," Cris murmured before realizing that she sounded like a house guest instead of the other way around. "I'm glad you've made yourself at home," she added as he opened the sports section of a day-old newspaper and buried himself behind it. When there was no response to her comment, she flounced over to her closet and put on a floor-length wool robe and slippers before heading downstairs for the shower.

Webb didn't emerge from the sports page then or ten minutes later, when she climbed back to the loft to get dressed in a pair of camel-colored slacks and an open-throated silk shirt of the same shade that just happened to be the newest items in her wardrobe.

She had to clear her throat to get his attention when she came down the stairs again. "Since you've already eaten breakfast, you'll excuse me if I go ahead with mine. Can I pour you another cup of coffee?"

The sports page came down then and was folded neatly on the table before he got to his feet. "You can get me a hell of a lot more than that."

Her mouth dropped open. "I beg your pardon?"

"I said that you can get me considerably more than a cup of coffee. I just had enough before to stave off starvation, since I didn't think you'd like me rooting around in your kitchen. Another ten minutes, though, and all my good intentions would have gone by the board."

She found herself on the defensive. "I'm sorry. You should have said something."

"I just did," he told her calmly, and leaned against the counter as she walked across to check the warmth of the coffeepot. "What's on the menu?"

"Eggs, bacon, toast—and grapefruit to start. How does that sound?"

"Couldn't be better." He reached to take a loaf of bread from her. "I'll manage this while you get cracking on the first course."

She couldn't resist correcting him. "The cracking comes with the eggs. The grapefruit we handle a little differently in this part of the country."

"I'll ignore that," he said, putting an egg carton on the counter before reaching for the frying pan from a copper hook behind the stove. "Any further discussion can be held after we eat. I presume there are plates and cups. . . ?"

"Right again," she told him blithely, finding it surprisingly delightful to share the breakfast chores rather than to stare at a bowl of cold cereal the way she usually did. "The plates and grapefruit will be ready whenever you are."

He nodded, switching the oven thermostat to "warm" and turning on the heat under the frying pan. Cristina watched a second longer before moving away to set two places at the breakfast bar which separated the cooking area from the end of the living room. Despite the gilded surroundings that Webb Colby frequented, he'd evidently been confronted with a kitchen stove and a cookbook sometime during his formative years.

At any rate, she could find no fault with the bacon omelettes which were served a little later. They both ate in a contented silence, unbroken except when she got up to make more toast and refill the coffee cups.

It wasn't until they were lingering over a third cup and the empty dishes were soaking in the sink that Webb pushed back his chair and asked, "What's on your agenda today? Anything special?"

His question caught Cris off-guard. "I—uh—I don't know. The usual thing, I suppose. Generally, I'm at work before this, but I doubt if there's much going on at the lodge this morning."

"Most of the inhabitants will still be sleeping it off," he agreed. "They're a good-natured bunch—I didn't hear a complaint from anybody last night."

"Probably they welcomed a break in the routine once they knew there was no danger. Before this, the staff talent show has been the highlight of the week's schedule, and it's a far cry from Las Vegas." She took another sip of coffee and then pushed the cup away. "I'd better go up to the lodge and see what progress is being made on those rooms—" She broke off as the telephone on the kitchen wall rang. "It's an extension from the lodge switchboard," she explained as she went over and lifted the receiver. "This is Cris. Mr. Colby? Yes, he's here," she told the operator. "Just a minute." She turned and held out the receiver. "For you," she said to Webb.

He came over to take it from her. "Colby here," he said into the mouthpiece. "Oh, good morning, William . . ."

His words made Cris pause in the process of clearing away the dishes. She could have sworn that it would be Sheila on the phone to find out when he'd be down to pick her up for the day. Shamelessly she eavesdropped on the rest of the conversation.

"No problems, eh? I'm glad to hear that you have it under control. All right, I'll tell her," Webb went on after a considerable pause. "Fine, thanks—I'd enjoy that very much."

Cris waited for his explanation after he hung up. When he simply started putting the butter dish into the refrigerator, whistling softly under his breath, she couldn't contain her curiosity any longer. "Tell me what?" she asked baldly.

He didn't pretend to misunderstand. "That you don't have to come in today. Brock said that he has the painters standing by but they can't do anything until the rooms are thoroughly dry. In the meantime, he's given you the day off. In a manner of speaking." The last sentence was tacked on significantly.

"Except there's a catch to it. Am I right?"

"Well, he seems to think somebody should make sure that I don't have a wasted weekend here at the lodge." Webb didn't try to hide the laughter in his voice.

The fact that he'd seen so clearly through the manager's stratagems made Cris forget about being diplomatic. "You can't blame Mr. Brock. He's doing his darndest to make sure that a favorable report gets back to the head office."

"But I don't have anything to do with the head office," Webb said, sounding as if he was getting tired of explaining. "I've never pretended to."

"Well, if you'd wanted to be completely ignored, you should have made sure that nobody recognized you when you checked in. Naturally Tom and Mr. Brock are rallying to save their paychecks."

"And you're not?"

Cris decided it wouldn't hurt him to know the truth about that. "I'm not depending on your good will to collect my pension, Mr. Colby. Naturally, I'm sorry that there was a mix-up in your room reservation and that you were inconvenienced by the fire—"

"But you're not shaking in your boots about any reports I might carry back to my mother." Webb walked over to retrieve his binoculars before continuing calmly. "And you certainly weren't enthusiastic to have me as a house guest last night. Isn't that right, Miss Kelly?"

"I'm sorry if you felt unwelcome," she replied stiffly, wondering what had happened to the friendly atmosphere of the breakfast table. "Frankly, I wasn't sure if you'd be comfortable over here."

"Very nicely put." He was stuffing the binoculars into a leather case he'd left on the fireplace mantel and didn't sound particularly interested in the way the conversation was going. "I'll be honest——my mother has been wanting me to come up this way

for some time. That's why I decided to have a
more comprehensive look at the property around
the lodge."

Cris felt an instant's sympathy for Mrs. Mathews'
efforts. How ridiculous that a grown man had to be
coerced into coming to see his inheritance!

It was fortunate that Webb still had his back
turned to her and didn't see her look of scorn.
"Brock doesn't think it's a good idea for me to
scout around on these trails alone," he was going
on, "so your services have been offered for the day.
Probably he meant it as a favor." His words trailed
off but there was no mistaking his meaning.

"You don't have to be polite about it," she
snapped. "I'm delighted to have a day off work and
we just won't tell him that you prefer going on
your own." Then feminine caution made her add,
"What trail did you plan to follow?"

"It's not important. Somebody mentioned that
the one to the ice caves was best for a day's
outing."

"Oh, no! That's much too difficult." The words
were out before Cris knew it. She saw the familiar
expression that was so disturbing settle over his
features and could have kicked herself for being
blunt. She started again. "The ice caves trail is
really for more experienced hikers. I think you'd
enjoy the walk to Reflection Lakes far more."

"I prefer the ice caves," Webb said, as if that
settled the matter.

Cristina desperately tried once more. "That path
hits seven thousand feet in places, and unless
you're in shape, the altitude can be very exhaust-
ing. We recommend that visitors start hiking at the
lower elevations and work up to trails with a

greater degree of difficulty. Why, I haven't been in that section all season myself."

"Then there's no reason for you to start now," Webb announced. "I'm sure Brock will understand."

Cristina's lips tightened ominously. William Brock *wouldn't* understand letting his prize guest go wandering off by himself, and no one knew it better than she did. Frightful visions of the Mountain Rescue Squad being mobilized to find Webb's missing body swept before her, along with a sequence of Army helicopters carrying back his broken form.

She took a deep breath and forced herself to say calmly, "It's out of the question for you to go alone. I'll be glad to accompany you. Actually I should check on some parts of the trail—most of it's Park Department property, but some of the land belongs to the lodge, so the upkeep is our responsibility." Her glance flickered over him thoughtfully as she spoke. His pants and shirt would be all right for the day's outing, but he'd do better with hiking shoes than with the loafers he was wearing. She opened her lips to suggest it, and then a perverse impulse made her close her mouth again. It wouldn't hurt him to suffer a little discomfort since he'd been so stubborn. That way, they'd have a much shorter day of it, and some newfound humility wouldn't be amiss when they got home again.

Webb merely said that he'd get his camera and be ready to leave shortlly. "I suppose we'll need some lunch if we're going to be gone more than an hour or so," he added after a pause.

"It's over six miles round trip, so we'd better have some food along," she agreed just as casually.

"I can carry it in a rucksack. Will a sandwich be all right with you?"

"Whatever you say," he told her as he started for the bedroom door. "Don't bother with much. I'm not particularly hungry."

Cristina took a stubborn delight in following his orders explicitly. She wasn't anxious to be burdened with any extra weight on the steep trail, and she was almost sure that they'd be back before lunch since the steepest part of the track was near the beginning. She would have bet her next month's salary that Webb would find an excuse to return to the lodge before climbing the first thousand feet.

With that in mind, she put together two cheese sandwiches with a careless hand, adding two apples, and a small box of raisins to the rucksack at the last minute. Webb was still behind the closed door of his bedroom when she went up the stairs to change.

It wasn't until she opened the door of her closet that she remembered her hiking boots were still waiting to be picked up at the shoe repair shop thirty miles away. She frowned—and decided it wouldn't hurt her to wear canvas shoes just this once. Fortunately the sky was cloudless, so they wouldn't have to worry about the possibility of rain. She would probably get wet feet if they reached the slushy ice of the cave area, but there was scant chance of that.

That conclusion buoyed her as she changed quickly into clean but worn jeans and short-sleeved cotton blouse. She hesitated over taking a sweater, wishing that she'd asked Yoshi and Kazy if they'd been troubled by mosquitos the day before. Impatiently she picked up a dark blue cardigan and then put it down again as she buttoned a plastic vial of bug repellent in her pocket. She was almost to the stairs before remembering a cotton brimmed hat, and she drew in a deep breath of disgust. Honestly! Anyone would think that she was the greenhorn around here.

The sharp peal of the telephone brought her out of the closet again and she was hurrying to the stairs when she heard the ringing slice off abruptly. She peered over the railing and saw that Webb had picked up the receiver. Even as she looked, he glanced upward and said, "Just a minute—I'll call her," into the mouthpiece and waggled the receiver at her significantly. "For you."

"Thanks." She clutched the hat in her hand as she hurried down the steps, wondering if Mr. Brock had had a change of mind about giving her the day off. "This is Cris," she said breathlessly when she took the phone.

"Hello, love." It was Tom Warden's deep voice on the wire. "I gather you still have your house guest."

She made a noncommittal murmur since the house guest at that moment was just three feet away and watching her with his arms folded casually over his chest. "How's the cleanup coming in the annex?" she asked, seeking a safer subject.

"All right, I guess. I've been busy with tax forms until now, when I decided I needed somebody to drink coffee with. Why don't you get rid of His Highness and come over to join me?"

"I'm afraid that won't be possible," she said, trying not to let Webb get the drift of the conversation.

"You mean it would be easier if I came over and

joined you?" Tom asked. "Tell me when the 'all clear' sounds and I can be there in three minutes."

Cris hugged the receiver to her ear. "You don't understand," she said, her color rising when she intercepted Webb's amused glance. "Mr. Brock has given me the day off."

"Great. I have some time coming, too. Why don't we make an afternoon of it. We can give Colby and his blonde plenty of leeway and no one will be any the wiser."

Cristina was so annoyed by then that she saw no point in trying to be diplomatic any longer. Let Webb think what he would. "Mr. Colby wants to see some of the lodge property today since the weather is so good. He thought he'd enjoy a short hike, and I'm going along to show him some of the landmarks."

"Oh, hell! I suppose old Bill is behind this shepherdess routine," Tom said bluntly. "Why can't Mrs. Simmons take care of her boy friend?" He clearly didn't expect any answer to that because he added irritably, "Well, that puts paid to any plans of ours unless you get back early this afternoon. Where are you taking him?"

"Mr. Colby thought he'd like to try the ice caves trail," she replied, and waited for his reaction.

It wasn't long in coming. "The ice caves!" he hooted incredulously, almost deafening her in the process. "Didn't you warn him, for pete's sake?"

Cris decided it was time to put a stop to the discussion before Webb became suspicious. "Thanks very much—I'm sure we will have since it's such a nice day," she said, making up the script as she went along. "I'll tell him you sent your best. 'Bye Tom." She hung up before he could reply, and turned to Webb. "That was Tom Warden. He . . ."

". . . sent his best," Webb finished drily. "Are you ready to go?" he asked, hoisting her rucksack with the lunch.

"I'll carry that," she said, reaching over to take it from his hands and looking around as she tried to remember if she'd forgotten anything. Tom's telephone call had only served to interrupt her train of thought. She unzipped the rucksack and surveyed its contents. "Lunch—hat—mosquito repellent"—the last was noted when she patted her shirt pocket—"I think that's everything. We might as well go before the trail gets too crowded."

Webb caught her halfway through the door with his gesture toward the mantelpiece. "Do those sunglasses up there belong to you? It's pretty bright outside—" he began, only to have her cut him off as she marched over to the fireplace.

"Of course," she said, snatching up the glasses and shoving them on her nose. "I don't know what I was thinking of."

"You'd have remembered before we got very far," he said calmly, shutting the chalet door behind them. "This way, we save a little time."

Cris shot a quick suspicious glance at him, wondering if he'd finally tumbled to the fact that the trip to the ice caves wasn't the quick forenoon outing he'd talked about.

Before she could attempt to find out, he was asking, "How far does the lodge property extend before we cross the park boundary?"

Cris was caught up in a lengthy explanation as they made their way past the big paved parking lot and joined a hard surfaced trail which cut through the open land in back of the lodge.

It was a beautiful morning, and the colorful alpine meadow around them was a fitting accompaniment to the cloudless sky. The snow-covered sides of the huge mountain dominated the panorama to their left while the lower peaks of the Cascade range showed evergreen-forested slopes to the south.

"Takes your breath away, doesn't it?" Webb said, stopping for a minute to enjoy the scenery. "No wonder the lodge is bursting at the seams this season. Do you know the names of those?" he asked, gesturing toward the wild flowers at the edge of the broad trail.

"A few," Cristina said as they walked on. "Those blue plants are lupines, the pink ones are heather, and those tall white clumps are called Indian Basket grass among other things. We have a nature lecture at the lodge this evening if you—and Mrs. Simmons—would like to attend."

"Sheila had other plans for the day. I doubt if she'll be available," Webb said, sounding regretful.

"Oh, I see." That was why he had time to go wandering around the landscape, Cristina decided with a sudden spurt of anger. When the silence between them lengthened, she continued in a stiff, formal tone. "You'll notice that we've posted signs to keep hikers off the meadows around here. The topsoil has been eroded by the bad weather over the years, and to counteract it, we replace the soil and put jute mesh over it to hold it in place. By the time that the mesh rots away, we hope the new vegetation has taken hold. Another method is to put turf 'plugs' in the distressed area, but it's difficult to make them work successfully."

When she paused to take a breath, Webb cut in, "I thought this was your day off."

Her eyes widened in surprise. "It is. Why?"

"Then there's no reason to act like a tour guide

to impress me. As a matter of fact, I read about this meadow conversion project on the bulletin board at the lodge last night." He reached in a back pocket of his pants for a nylon cap with a deep bill to shade his eyes. "The sun feels as if it might get hot around midday," he said mildly.

Cristina didn't respond. She was still smarting over his earlier comment, knowing that he saw it for what it was—a glib recital of statistics to parade her knowledge. With that sobering thought going 'round in her head, it dawned on her that Webb had made a few changes to his outfit while she had been getting ready. He was wearing a pair of jeans that looked well-worn and comfortable plus a cotton shirt with long sleeves casually rolled to the elbows. She also noted the pair of far-from-new hiking shoes he was wearing, and she frowned thoughtfully as he fished a bandana from his other pants pocket and started to polish his sunglasses with it.

Cristina was following his movements so closely that she would have wandered off the edge of the trail if his hand hadn't shot out suddenly and pulled her back. "Watch it! You'd have been in that thorn bush in another minute," he warned. Then as he dropped his grip, he flexed his hand significantly. "You've already picked up your quota of prickles, haven't you, Cristina? Don't tell me you're going to sulk for the rest of the day. Why not try for a happy medium? Something between a tour conductor and the great stone face. There's no reason to act like the world's coming to an end because you had to turn Warden down this one time."

Cris almost blurted out that Tom had nothing to do with her behavior and then realized that it was far safer to remain silent on that score. If Webb didn't realize that his presence was the reason for her turbulent feelings, she'd come through in better shape.

By that time, they'd reached the end of the meadow—and the end of the wide, hard-surfaced trail as well. The latter changed to a dirt track barely wide enough for one person as it wound its way upward around the hillside.

They paused for a moment to admire the clear water of Myrtle Falls falling away to the right of them, and then Cristina gestured across to a sharp ridge directly ahead, where a few hikers could be seen nearing the top. "The lodge property ends at the base of that cliff, and the Park Department maintains the trail from there on up to the caves."

Webb's eyes were thoughtful slits as he looked across the valley into the sun. "I imagine this meadow and that stand of timber down below the falls might be pretty valuable."

"I suppose so." She tried to hide her annoyance at his commercial outlook. "We've never considered any logging around the lodge. People have come to see the wild flowers in these meadows ever since I can remember. That's why we've worked so hard to preserve them."

"I thought there was some discussion about putting in ski lifts and developing the property for a winter sports center. Or maybe I have it wrong . . ." He turned to look down at her.

"No," she acknowledged reluctantly, "a development company did make an offer. My grandfather was against selling any of the property as a matter of principle. I don't know about your mother's feelings on the project."

Webb shrugged. "I have no idea. There weren't

any lengthy discussions about it that I can remember."

"Probably because you had other interests."

"And still do." His glance slid over her again as if he'd caught the sarcasm in her tone and was merely amused by it. "Well, let's keep going, shall we? I'd rather get over the steepest part of the trail before the sun gets any hotter."

She held back for an instant. "I thought you didn't know anything about hiking."

"That's merely common sense. Besides, I don't need to worry about such details today—Brock made sure that I was well taken care of." He started off, saying over his shoulder, "I'll go ahead for now. When we come to the steep part of the trail, I'll let you take over and pull me along."

Cristina would have argued or at least uttered a scathing comment, but by that time she had to hurry to keep up with his lengthy stride. A few minutes later, she was still hurrying—strictly from choice. It didn't take long to discover that the past week of hot August weather had made the dirt of the trail powder-dry. Even the lightest footstep brought it up in a choking cloud, so that Cristina, relegated to squaw's position behind Webb, found herself in a constant screen of dust.

The only way to avoid it was to follow closely on his heels before the silt had a chance to rise. As simple as the solution seemed, Cristina found it impossible to keep up with his long-legged pace. She was breathing rapidly and starting to perspire although they were on the level part of the trail and still within sight of the steep cedar roof of the lodge.

Suddenly Webb pulled up in the shade of a subalpine fir and cocked his head to listen. Cristina came up beside him, wanting to rest on a nearby boulder but liking the tree's shade even more. She managed to lean against the trunk as she reached for a handkerchief to mop her face.

"There he is," Webb said, pointing at the steep hillside above the trail. "Right at the base of that hemlock."

Cris looked up, startled. "There's who?"

"A marmot. Didn't you hear him whistle?" Webb's attention was on the big rodent who was staring just as intently down at them. "There must be plenty of food around this season—he certainly hasn't missed any meals in the last month or so." Cristina managed a noncommittal murmur, bringing Webb's glance down again. "You look warm," he said in a surprised tone of discovery. "Better put on a hat or your nose will be even redder in another hour or so. You did bring a hat, didn't you?"

"Of course I brought one," she retorted crossly, glad that she had the right answer for once. She scrabbled in the rucksack and pulled it out. It wasn't until she was putting it on that something else registered, and she stiffened with incredulity.

"What's the matter?" Webb asked almost immediately, showing that very little was escaping his gaze on either the hillside or the trail.

"Why—nothing," she managed, smoothing the brim of her hat unnecessarily. There was no need to volunteer the information that she'd just then discovered that she'd left her sweater back at the chalet. Actually it probably wouldn't matter, since there wasn't a cloud in the sky. The worst that could happen would be getting her arms sunburned, but that wouldn't prove fatal. She looked up again and encountered Webb's quizzical gaze. "What are we waiting for?" she asked.

He ran his thumb along his jawbone as he stared back at her. Then he shrugged. "Damned if I know. Maybe you'd rather take the lead this time."

There was nothing in his tone to indicate that he was aware of her difficulties before, Cristina decided, and smiled in some relief. "All right. The trail's still level for another half mile, so we might as well take it easy and conserve our energy."

"That sounds sensible. It's a good thing you're along."

She did risk a suspicious glance at him after that remark, but he was surveying the valley below, his expression impassive as usual.

The next half mile was easier. The dust was no problem for Cris and Webb kept so closely on her heels that he apparently wasn't bothered either. She would liked to have wet her face in an icy stream which they crossed, but another hiking party was taking up the convenient bank just then. Since Webb showed no disposition to linger, she took a deep breath and set out on the narrow dirt track which wound steeply upward from that point.

Once away from the mountain stream, an almost primeval silence settled about them. There was a hot baked smell from the rust-colored earth beneath their feet as the midday sun blazed down on the zigzag trail. Dust rose almost apathetically behind them, settling again to coat the leaves of the huckleberry and lupine which clung precariously to the rocky hillside. As they neared the first switchback, a raven uttered a throaty protest as it soared from a branch in a clump of trees up into the cloudless sky.

Cristina lingered in the shade of the curved tree trunks, enjoying even a brief respite from the sun's rays. She tried to think of a reason to prolong the stop and fell back on her tour guide status. "You'll notice how most of the trees on the hillside follow this same angle," she told Webb as he moved over beside her. His eyebrows rose quizzically, but he didn't say anything so she continued with the lecture, trying to sound offhand about it. "The growth pattern occurs when the trees are young and vulnerable to the winter snow cover as it creeps down the slopes. When the warm weather comes around in the summer, they start growing upright again. In the meantime—"

"In the meantime, I think you'd do better to save your breath," Webb cut in. "There's still a ways to go," he added, jerking his head toward the next steep switchback. "Or hadn't you noticed?"

The temperature had already given her a heightened color, so that he wasn't able to gauge the effect of his words. "Sorry—I didn't mean to bore you," she said, trying to hide her annoyance. "I'm ready whenever you are."

Something about Webb's expression as he gestured her forward showed that he found her forbearance even more irritating than her nature talks. For an instant, Cris wondered at his reaction, and then she was too busy trying to conserve her energy for the steep climb to think of anything else.

It took them a half hour more of steady climbing to get to the end of the switchbacks and finally reach the ridge. This time, even Webb didn't object as Cris collapsed on a flat rock at the trail's edge to wait for her heart to stop pounding. He simply sat down on another rock and reached for his camera to photograph the awe-inspiring peaks of the Tatoosh range. After pushing the shutter twice, he capped the lens and seemed content to rest while admiring the scenery. Five minutes went by in a relaxed silence before he turned to Cris. "Haven't you anything to say about the granodiorite being scratched by the flow of the glacier or the orange soil caused by the ash eruption from Mount Mazama?"

She looked steadily back at him. "I suppose I'll find out eventually that you wrote the booklet we give our guests. Have you finished playing games with all of us, Mr. Colby, or is there more in store—and don't pretend that you don't know what I'm talking about. This isn't the first trail you've been on." Her voice rose angrily. "Why, you aren't even breathing hard."

"Is that bad? After all, you brought the whole thing about. You decided that the only thing I'd ever climbed was a ladder on the side of a swimming pool and I didn't want to argue with you. It's too bad you aren't in better shape yourself."

His taunt brought Cris to her feet as if she'd been stung. "I'll show you who's in shape. There's still a long way to go, so if you're ready . . ."

For a minute, it looked as if he was going to protest. Then he shrugged and got to his feet. "I'm ready. Let me know when you want to stop for lunch," was the sum total of his reply.

After that, there was no more conversation. The narrow trail leveled off as it followed the ridge for a distance. Unfortunately, the loose dirt surface worked its way into Cristina's canvas shoes along with enough grit to make her feel that she was walking barefoot through a gravel pit after a while. She stopped and emptied them when she couldn't bear it any longer and in the process became aware that a blister was forming on her right heel.

Webb leaned against a tree with his hands in his pockets as he waited, but he kept discreetly silent. Cristina's expression became more determined than ever as she retied her shoes and they started off again.

At the end of another lengthy interval, they reached the edge of a moraine, a vast wasteland of rocks dumped by the glacier. Cristina forgot her physical discomfort as she considered announcing that the rocks were approximately eleven thousand years old, just to see if Webb could be tempted into another scathing reply. By then, she would have done almost anything to shake him out of his polite silence.

Fortunately the decision was taken from her. Webb moved over to the edge of the trail before it widened onto the rock-studded plateau and jerked his thumb toward a clump of hemlock some fifteen feet ahead of them. "If we want lunch in the shade, we'd better take what's offered. All right with you?"

Cris grasped the olive branch eagerly. "I'm starved," she agreed, and wasted no time in getting to the hemlocks and sinking to her knees. "I wish now that I'd made thicker sandwiches or taken more time with the filling."

"Right now, any kind of sandwich sounds great," Webb said, watching her swing the rucksack off her back. "An innerspring mattress wouldn't come amiss, either." He looked around for somewhere to hang his cap and then stuck it on a protruding branch near his elbow.

The acknowledgment that he had a few aching muscles of his own cheered Cris immeasurably. Suddenly the prospect of a shared picnic lunch with the tall man sprawled out on the shady bit of ground beside her lost its frightening qualities and she started to relax.

Unzipping the rucksack, she brought out the sandwiches in their plastic wrap and gave them to Webb to hold while she delved into the interior again and found the apples and raisins. "I'm not sure about the order of the menu," she said, dividing the provisions in two neat piles. "But at least we should manage to keep body and soul together until we get back to the chalet."

Webb smiled and unbuttoned a deep shirt pocket, hauling out two candy bars which he added to the picnic fare. "My contribution. It never hurts to have a few more calories."

After that, they ate in a contented silence, broken only when two parties of hikers passed them and stopped to exchange pleasantries. The last group were on their way down the trail after visiting the ice caves. They volunteered the information that there was a good hour's hike still ahead for Webb and Cristina.

"I don't envy you, either," one of the men told them frankly. "Crossing the moraine in this weather is like going across Death Valley." He let his gaze linger on Cris's forearms. "Looks to me as if you'd gotten a pretty good sunburn already."

"I've been trying to get a decent tan all summer," she told him blithely, but wishing that he'd mind his own business. Webb had shoved his sunglasses up on his forehead at the remark and was now giving her a clinical look.

He waited, however, until the men had gone on their way down the trail before he said mildly, "That fellow was right. You'd better haul out a jacket or something to cover those arms."

"Sorry, I'm fresh out," she said flippantly, not

meeting his eyes as she started to clear away the wrappings from their sandwiches and candy bars.

"You mean you came on this with nothing to protect your arms?" The annoyed note was back in his voice. "My god, I thought you knew better than that!"

"I *did* have a sweater out to bring, but the telephone rang about then and in the confusion—I forgot to put it in. When I realized, it was too late to go back."

"Well, it's not too late now." There was a decisive bite to his words. "Another few hours in this sunshine and you'll be crisp."

"That's ridiculous!" Cris wanted to tell him that she was far more worried about the blister on her heel. Imagining his reaction to that almost made her burst out laughing. The whole thing was absurd anyway, she decided. Her assignment to supervise Webb Colby made as much sense as sending a physical education teacher to guide Sir Edmund Hillary. Then she came back to the present as Webb's conversation penetrated.

"There's nothing ridiculous about it," he was saying, zipping up the rucksack and tossing it on his shoulder as he got to his feet. "Let's get going. Right now."

He bent over to retrieve his cap so he missed the mutinous expression that came over Cristina's face. Any other approach and she would have meekly agreed. Even if he'd announced that the weather was too warm to make the ice caves worth the bother, she would have gone along with the fiction. But that overbearing, dictatorial pronouncement which overruled the slightest objection on her part sent Cris's common sense flying.

"You can go wherever you choose," she said just

as definitely, leaving little doubt as to where she'd consign him if she had a choice. "I came to see the ice caves and that's what I intend to do. Unless you think you'll have trouble finding your way back to the lodge alone."

She saw his fingers clench at his side and felt a thrill of satisfaction. Aside from tossing her over his shoulder, which was hardly possible on the narrow, winding trail, there wasn't a damned thing he could do but seethe.

It became abruptly obvious that he didn't intend to give her that satisfaction for long. "I don't anticipate any trouble whatsoever," he said, his voice sounding as icy as the glacier looming above them on the side of the mountain. "Enjoy your hike."

Cristina watched him start down the trail and then found her vision blurred with the tears which suddenly filled her eyes. She reached up and pulled her hat down more securely in the only gesture of defiance she could make before turning to start in the other direction.

It was on her second step that she committed the cardinal sin of not watching to see where she was going. As she mopped her eyes, she caught her foot on a protruding tree root and promptly sprawled at full length on the rocky ground.

"Oh!" She let out an involuntary shriek which changed to a painful moan as her rib cage came to rest against a sharp-edged rock. For an instant she lay where she had fallen, still dazed from the impact. Then, even as she began to push herself erect, she felt a strong arm go around her and a familiar masculine voice saying, "Hold still! Don't try to move until I can see if you've done any damage."

"I think you'll find the rock's still in good shape,"

she managed, sitting up despite his orders. Thankfully, his clasp didn't lessen and she leaned against him shamelessly as she waited for the landscape to stop going up and down.

Then she became conscious of a dampness on her blouse and winced as she gingerly felt her ribs. "It feels as if something *is* wrong somewhere."

Webb said something in an explosive undertone and unbuttoned her blouse with firm but gentle fingers, pushing aside her hand in the process.

"You don't have to do that . . ." she objected.

"Be quiet." He didn't raise his voice, but there was something in his tone that prevented further argument.

After his fingers probed her bare midriff, she finally decided that she had a few privileges left. "I'm perfectly all right, I tell you. Nothing hurts when I breathe—" She broke off sharply as his exploring hand touched a painful spot.

"Not much it doesn't," he said grimly and daubed his handkerchief against her grazed skin.

"You know what I mean," she said, wishing she could simply dissolve in tears the way unliberated females once had a right to do.

Webb let out a ragged sigh of relief which showed that his air of composure was a little thin, too. "You've scraped off some of your top layer but it shouldn't keep you out of a bikini very long. The main thing now is to get you back to the lodge and clean you up a bit. Can you manage to walk?"

Cristina caught the worried undercurrent and she tacked on a determined smile. "Absolutely. I refuse to be propped against a rock and abandoned in this place."

"That's the girl." Webb left her shirttail hanging outside her belt but he buttoned her blouse and helped her up. "We can sponge off the dirt once we get down to the stream."

"Exactly whose dirt are 'we' sponging off? Ours or mine?"

"You must be feeling better," he said in a resigned tone. "I'm surprised that you're not still intent on detouring by the ice caves before you give in."

Since he was steering her firmly down the trail while he spoke, Cristina didn't bother to rise to the bait. Even the first few steps had shown her that the trip back down the trail would take every bit of will power that she could summon.

"When Mr. Brock hears about this, I'll never live it down," she said, only half-joking. "And you'll be entitled to ask for a refund on the weekend."

Webb shot her a quizzical sideways glance and his arm tightened almost imperceptibly around her shoulders. "You've already donated a pound of flesh," he said. "I'm quite satisfied with that."

Chapter Five

◆◆◆◆◆◆◆◆◆◆◆◆◆◆◆◆◆◆◆◆◆◆◆◆◆◆◆◆◆◆◆◆

The grueling walk back down the trail blurred into one painfully long passage of time.

Cris tried to avoid jarring her bruised rib cage, and Webb helped by keeping a firm grip on her shoulders and walking alongside whenever the path was wide enough. By then, the blister on her heel felt even more fiery than her midriff, but she managed to keep from limping until they finally got down to the creek after negotiating the steep part of the trail.

There was an ominous angle to Webb's jaw when he led her to a boulder on the bank. "Sit down there," he said, "and shed that blouse. After that, you can take off the shoe."

"I'll wait until I get back home," she began, only to have him interrupt brusquely.

"The sooner the dirt's out of those grazes the better," he announced, getting out his handkerchief again.

Her hands went reluctantly to the buttons of her blouse. "What if someone comes along?" she began, knowing she couldn't very well complain about his presence. Not without having her head taken off. The assured way that he'd stripped off her blouse at the top of the trail showed that he hadn't given it a second thought.

77

"Oh, for god's sake! The sight of a woman in a bra might shock a stray chipmunk or two, but frankly I can't think of anybody else."

Without another word, she unbuttoned her blouse while he dampened his handkerchief in the icy water. She drew in her breath sharply when he started gently cleansing the scratches on her chest and then remained motionless until he'd finished.

"Now take off your shoe," he ordered.

This time, she knew better than to protest and meekly accepted the handkerchief after she'd bathed her blistered heel in the stream.

He watched with narrowed eyes while she fashioned a pad from it inside her shoe and then helped her on with her blouse. When she fumbled with its buttons, he made an annoyed sound and pushed her hand aside to finish the job himself. It was impossible to tell what he was thinking, and, after sneaking an upward look, Cris hurriedly lowered her own glance once again.

After that, there was no more discussion until they finally reached the lodge parking lot considerably later that afternoon. At least not until Webb tried to steer her to the path leading to the lobby entrance of the resort.

"I'm not going in there," Cris said, pulling up abruptly and ignoring the curious stares of some hikers who were passing at the moment.

"Then where in the hell do you think you're going?" If Webb was relieved that they'd finally reached the end of the trail, it didn't show in his clipped words.

"I'm going home, that's where." Cris wished that she had enough strength to turn and stride off alone after her declaration but she knew that she'd founder right there in the middle of the parking lot if she tried it.

Webb knew it too. For an instant, she thought he was going to call her bluff. Then his expression softened as he relented. "Okay—home it is."

He kept his arm around her waist as he led her through the rows of parked campers and groups of chattering visitors. Cristina managed to hide the worst part of her blouse and was grateful that they were accepted as two more grimy hikers in a place where dirt was scarcely a novelty.

Webb's casual air disappeared as soon as they got inside the door of the chalet. He took one look at Cristina's pale exhausted face and swept her up in his arms.

When she opened her eyes again, she was lying on his bed in the guest bedroom. Webb had disappeared, but when she started to sit up, he reappeared with a basin of hot water and a first-aid box. Her blouse was peeled off again without comment before he started to work.

His touch was deft and impersonal as he made sure the abraded skin was clean, finally applying plastic bandages to the two deepest grazes. It was afterward, when he was reaching across to remove the basin of water, that his hand accidentally brushed the gentle curve of her breast. She gasped audibly and felt her cheeks turn a fiery red. An instant later she was hoping desperately that he hadn't noted her reaction.

If he had, he didn't let on. All he said was, "I'll toss in a pair of pajamas for you. The rest of those scratches shouldn't bleed so there's no need to bandage them. I'll take care of your heel after you've gotten undressed." He paused at the door of the bedroom. "Can you manage okay."

Cristina had to clear her throat before she could answer. "Yes—yes, of course."

"All right then—get cracking."

Minutes later the door was opened again and a pair of pajamas landed unceremoniously on the bed. "I'll give you five minutes," Webb announced from the hallway, and then Cris heard his footsteps retreating.

That time, she got off the bed and went over to lock the door behind him. Unfortunately, he was running water in the kitchen by then, so he missed her defiant gesture. She frowned even more deeply as she surveyed the pajamas he'd found. She might have known he'd choose her best white Dior pair with a persimmon trim when she looked like a bedraggled refugee.

All Webb really noticed when he returned were the lingering traces of exhaustion still visible in her translucent complexion and her shadowed eyes. He handed her a steaming cup of tea as she sat propped up against the pillows with a down comforter pulled up to her breast. "I'm glad to see that you're finally showing some sense," he said, with an approving glance. "If you get some of this tea inside you, you can have something stronger in a little while. Now stick out your foot—I have a bandage for that blister."

"I can't stay here on top of your bed," she protested halfheartedly as she settled against the pillows again a little later.

"I don't know why not—unless you want me to ask Brock over as a chaperone. Or would your friend Tom suit you better?"

Cristina recognized the gentle probing and took a minute to reply. If she told the truth about her friendship with Tom, it stripped her of any defense for the future, and the accountant could prove to be a valuable buffer when Sheila reappeared in Webb's picture. "You're the one who's being ridiculous now," she said quietly. "Tom trusts me completely."

The way that Webb's eyes narrowed showed that he recognized her evasiveness. "You have him better trained than I thought."

"That's a miserable thing to say . . ."

"Forget it. You don't have to worry. I observe all of the rules—and they don't include seducing an unwilling hostess no matter whose bed she's on. Are you feeling any better?"

His quick change of subject made Cris frown in sudden confusion. "I—I—think so. The tea tastes good. But I'm perfectly capable of . . ."

". . . getting to your own bed," he finished for her. "I wish to god that you'd drag your mind to another subject. Frankly, I think it's time that we stopped playing games and started leveling with each other."

She felt a stab of apprehension that was as painful as her bruised ribs. "I don't know what you're talking about. I've told you the truth . . ."

"As far as it goes." He sat down on the foot of the bed and propped his back against the wall. "Maybe you haven't read the lodge balance sheet for the last two quarters."

"Of course I have. I admitted that we'd had trouble. Expensive trouble. But now Mr. Brock hopes that we can recoup some of the losses by the end of the season." She broke off as a sudden thought struck her. "Wait a minute—I thought you didn't have any interest in the lodge. You have a nerve accusing *me* of playing games. *You're* the one who's here under false pretenses."

"Nothing of the sort," Webb growled, but he stirred uneasily as if trying to find a more comfortable position on the mattress. "I can't help it if you and Brock started leaping to all the wrong conclusions."

"You didn't deny them. If I'd had any sense, I'd have tumbled to your charade before the hike today." Her gaze became speculative. "Exactly what *do* you do for a living?"

"I'm an engineer." The words came out almost unwillingly.

"That covers a multitude of sins."

"I don't deny it. Let's just say that I look after the family interests among other things."

"You mean that your mother has other properties like this one?"

"And my stepfather," he acknowledged. "I've been out of the country for a while—that's why I haven't kept in touch on the lodge here. I can tell you this, though—another year like this last one and the place will be a monumental white elephant. Nobody but a fool would keep ploughing capital back in," he added severely.

Seeing the stubborn line of his jaw, Cristina wondered how she could ever have cast him in the role of an indulged dilettante. The lack of emotion in his voice showed that any decisions he made for his family would be based solely on sound business principles reinforced with a profit and loss statement.

"Fortunately," he was going on, "there's always the value of the land. That's fairly simple to reckon. Afterward we can weigh the financial advantages of selling for the timber rights or for property development. There have been offers from companies on both sides."

His hard-hearted disposal of the property she'd loved for so long cut into Cris like an edge of cold steel.

Webb's expression relaxed as he noticed her distress. "I'm sorry if this sounds too cut and dried, but that's why your grandfather left the final disposition of the property up to my mother. He wanted to make sure that your interests would be protected before anything else. Probably he suspected that you'd invest your last cent in this place just because of some sentimental memories."

"So you knew about the wording of the trust all along." Cristina's eyebrows drew together in an ominous line. "I hope you had fun with your cat and mouse tactics. Was it necessary for you to come on quite so strong?"

His mouth tightened. "I just followed the role that you'd allotted me." He got to his feet as he went on. "And I have no intention of making any final decision about the place without discussing it first, so you can drop that injured air. Frankly, I didn't even want to get mixed up in this. If I had my way, the property would be divided, and you could do what you want with your section." He leaned over to take the empty tea mug from her unresisting fingers and put it on the bedside table. "I can assure you that playing god isn't my idea of how to spend the first time off I've had in months."

His brusque statement was all she needed to cap that terrible afternoon. "I'm sorry that you've been inconvenienced," she managed, swinging her feet to the floor. "At least, we don't have to pretend any longer." By then, she realized that he hadn't bothered to bring slippers along with her pajamas, nor had she thought to request a robe. "I'm going up to bed now. There's no reason for you to stay around any longer if you'd like to drive down and visit Mrs. Simmons."

He ignored that suggestion completely, merely saying irritably, "My good girl, you can't walk around barefooted on this cold floor."

"I am *not* your good girl," she informed him, wondering if she'd have to push him out of the way in order to reach the door. Her chin took on a defiant angle. "Frankly, I don't think even you're capable of carrying me up a spiral staircase, so"—she made an airy brushing motion with her hand—"just move aside."

There wasn't time to evade his next move even if she'd known what was going to happen. One moment she was standing in front of him and the next he had simply hoisted her against his chest like a four-year-old. She was still rigid with surprise as he pulled open the bedroom door and started toward the front of the chalet. By the time she gasped, "Stop it! Put me down this minute!"—he was out in the living room.

His tightened grip around her hips was his only answer as he started up the stairs to the loft. She had the disturbing suspicion that if her rib cage wasn't already bruised, she'd have been tossed over his shoulder in true cave-man style. After that, she didn't dare struggle as he climbed steadily up the narrow iron stairs, waiting instead until he put her down unceremoniously on the floor by the edge of her bed.

He must have had an inkling of her intentions then, because his hand shot out and caught her wrist on the way up. "I wouldn't recommend it," he drawled. "For one thing, I'm bigger and you wouldn't stand a chance if I decided to hit back.

Besides, I was just doing my good deed for the day."

By then, Cris was so furious that she had trouble keeping her breathing under control. His grip on her wrist felt like steel, and every nerve end in her body was still pulsing from the close contact on that trip up the stairs. She could only hope that her pounding heartbeat wasn't visible through the thin fabric of her pajama top. "Just go away, will you? If you don't, I swear I'll . . ."

"You'll what?" He sounded genuinely interested; only the mockery in his eyes gave away his amusement. "I don't know what you're so upset about. I've probably saved you from a case of pneumonia or a miserable cold, at least. Call it self-preservation if you like. After all, we're going to share the same roof for a while."

"*Will* you let go of me," she hissed, trying to shake off his hold.

His clasp loosened slightly but not enough for her to free herself. "Nobody told me that you had such a nasty temper," he went on in a thoughtful tone, as if he'd just uncovered a rare scientific find. "And it's obvious that I don't seem to be making any headway with a logical approach, so there's really just one other way."

His words were so deliberate that Cristina was unprepared for what happened next. Without a waste motion, she was pulled against his tall form so fast that she gasped. When she started to protest, her chin was tilted up and secured in a firm grip. Then with every evidence of masculine enjoyment, his mouth came down to cover hers.

At the beginning of that kiss, Cristina's emotions exploded like a fireworks display on the Fourth of July. Her last fleeting thought of resistance collapsed as the kiss deepened. When Webb's arms moved over her back, she instinctively let him mold her body against his.

It was only the need to breathe which made her eventually push away, and she stood clinging to the front of his shirt, her heartbeat sounding like a marathon competitor's. She finally risked an upward glance when Webb stepped back and let her go. There was a tight look on his face—almost as if he regretted what he'd done. Cris recalled the way she'd capitulated and suddenly wished she could disappear on the spot instead of having to think of something inconsequential to say.

As it turned out, she was spared that. Webb hesitated just a minute longer, then turned on his heel and started for the stairs. "I think you'd better get to bed," he said over his shoulder. "It's been a hell of a day. I'll see you in the morning."

He'd vanished down the steps almost before he finished speaking, and a moment later, Cris heard the door to the guest bedroom slam with a decided finality.

For an instant, she stood where she was and let her confused emotions flood over her. Then slowly—moving like a mesmerized robot—she got into bed and resolutely closed her eyes. A hell of a day was putting it mildly.

Chapter Six

◆◆◆◆◆◆◆◆◆◆◆◆◆◆◆◆◆◆◆◆◆◆◆◆◆◆◆

After what happened, it was surprising that Cris managed to sleep at all. It was even more surprising that she fell asleep almost as soon as her head touched the pillow and didn't waken until nine the next morning.

She stared unbelievingly at the alarm clock and then threw back the covers to get out of bed. As soon as one foot reached the floor, however, her stiff and sore muscles protested.

Then everything came flooding back—the ice cave trail with all its hazards and later that chastising kiss which Webb had forced upon her.

Honesty made her acknowledge that "forced" was scarcely the proper word. Her eager cooperation must have been a surprise to both of them. Otherwise, why would Webb have made an exit that was more of a rout than a retreat?

That remembrance brought a frown, and she carefully pulled on a robe before going to peer over the railing into the room below.

The deserted living area presented two possibilities; Webb was either still asleep or had left the chalet without breakfast. When she went downstairs, she found that her latter suspicion was correct. The kitchen was immaculate and the bed in his room had been neatly made. Only his closed suitcase on the racks showed that she had a house guest at all.

Cristina's first feeling of relief wore away. She bathed gingerly before donning slacks and a comfortable linen overblouse, and after that, she went into the kitchen only to turn away again as she reached the refrigerator. Somehow the thought of food had lost its appeal and she decided to settle for a sweet roll and coffee when she reached the lodge.

She was halfway through the front door by the time she realized that a linen blouse wasn't warm enough for her journey across to the big building. Overnight, the temperature had plunged downward as if in sympathy with her mood. Even the color of the mountain had changed to a monochrome, with the sides shrouded in a gray mist and darker gray clouds gathering ominously at the summit. Those weather signs—along with the southerly breeze called a Chinook which was already bending flowers alongside the walk—were sure indicators of rain in the near future.

So much for their peak summer season. Cris pulled up the zipper of her nylon windbreaker and tucked her chin into the quilted collar of the jacket as she walked along, wondering whether Webb would use the changing weather as an excuse for cutting short his stay. Her lips tightened when she realized she was imagining things again. A single kiss certainly wouldn't affect a mature person one way or the other. It hadn't had any noticeable effect on her. While she was reaching that decision, she passed Kazy on the lodge porch without speaking, and then told a perfect stranger that it was nice to see him again.

It took Yoshi's hail from behind the desk to bring her back to normal. "Cris—what are you doing here?"

Cristina's eyebrows came together in a frown. "That's a silly question. I'm working, of course."

"But you're not supposed to be working." The diminutive desk clerk leaned over the counter with a concerned expression. "You're supposed to be in bed at the chalet. Mr. Colby told us what happened yesterday when he came in for breakfast." She saw Cris turn automatically toward the dining room and added, "He's not there now. He left already."

"He can't have left—his bags are still at the house." Cris broke off when she noticed Yoshi's black eyes gleam with interest. "At least, they were five minutes ago," she added, trying to sound as if it didn't matter one way or the other.

"I just meant that he's gone out for the day. He had breakfast with Mr. Brock and told him that you'd be taking the day off."

"How did he know that? I didn't even see him this morning."

Her indignant denial didn't surprise Yoshi. "I know," she said soothingly. "He didn't want to wake you—apparently you were still sleeping soundly when he left. Mr. Colby even arranged for Tom to take you down to the doctor for X-rays this afternoon."

"He *has* been busy." Cris gave a fleeting look at her watch. "It isn't even ten o'clock. I'm glad that I didn't sleep till noon. Lord knows what would have been decreed by then!"

Yoshi was crestfallen at her reaction. "I thought he was wonderful. And he was terribly concerned.

At least that's what Mr. Brock said. I heard him talking to Tom afterward."

Cris wanted to ask why she was being parceled out if Webb was so concerned, but she knew better. All she said was, "Did Mr. Colby mention when he'd be back?"

"Not to me. I thought he might have told you last night—before you went to bed."

"No, he didn't say anything." Cris couldn't hide her stricken reaction as she remembered some of the other things Webb had accomplished without conversation the night before. Her own actions were still appallingly clear in her mind, too—her unquestioning surrender at the outset, the shameless way she had responded to his touch, even her reluctance to leave his arms. Surely Webb hadn't been regaling the lodge staff with a detailed account of all that.

Yoshi's expression sobered when she saw her unhappy face. "He *did* stay overnight at the chalet, didn't he?" she reiterated.

"Oh—that. Yes, of course."

The desk clerk reached across to gently pat her hand. "Cris, honey—why don't you go and have some coffee. Right now I don't think you're playing with a full deck."

Cristina's lips twitched in an unwilling smile. "Full deck, indeed! You've been around Kazy too long. Heaven knows what kind of English he'll teach you when you're married."

"I plan on doing a little teaching myself," Yoshi said smugly. "That crazy Kazy thinks that you and I are F.O.B. where men are concerned."

Cris had started to walk away but she pulled up. "And exactly what does F.O.B. mean?"

"Fresh off the boat." Yoshi's dark eyes were sparkling. "That means—"

"I know what that means," Cris cut in. "Even in my weakened state. Now I'm going to have some breakfast, and after that, I'm going back to bed again. Kazy would probably say that I'm retreating from the world."

"It sounds like a wonderful idea to me. Shall I tell Tom where you are?"

"If he asks," Cris said drily. "I don't plan to take the phone off the hook. Since he's been inveigled into the ambulance run, I might as well cooperate."

"You don't sound happy about it."

"That's because I haven't had breakfast," Cris said lightly. "I never sound happy in the morning. Probably that's the reason Mr. Colby left the chalet so early."

"No, it wasn't that. He was looking forward to keeping an appointment with Mrs. Simmons this morning." Yoshi stopped as she saw the other's lips tighten. "I'm sorry, Cris—I just happened to overhear his phone call to her."

"Forget it. After all, the man's a free agent." Cris managed a creditable smile. "Call me at the chalet if you have any problems."

After that, she headed for a deserted corner of the dining room to eat her breakfast, hoping that food would help her. She determinedly hid behind a newspaper while she toyed with a poached egg on toast, deciding that even the headline announcing a new tax raise was better than her thoughts at the moment.

The phone was ringing when she got back to the chalet after breakfast and she hurried to answer it.

"Cristina?" It was Tom's voice. "Yoshi told me that I just missed you. Why didn't you let me know that you were eating at the lodge? I would have joined you."

"I'm sorry. It didn't occur to me that you'd be interested." She took a tighter grip on the receiver as she added, "I understand that you've been drafted to take me for X-rays this afternoon, but it really isn't necessary."

"Maybe not for you, but it is for me," he replied, chuckling. "Brock would tie me to a stake if I didn't. I was there when he confirmed the appointment. So was Colby."

"But I feel all right," she argued, ignoring the fact that she'd discovered at least ten aching muscles she hadn't even known she possessed. "Honestly, there isn't any reason for X-rays."

"That's not the way Colby talked this morning." Tom adopted a businesslike tone. "It's probably a good idea to avoid taking any chances."

"All right, then." She decided it was time to stop fighting the inevitable. "Would you rather go down to the hospital this morning? I have the whole day off, so it doesn't matter to me."

There was a pause while Tom cleared his throat. "Well, actually, I had made other plans for the forenoon."

"Then we'll stick to the original schedule. Just tell me what time to be ready."

"I thought we could leave about four. After you're through at the hospital, we can have dinner in the village. How does that sound?"

Cris tried to match his enthusiasm. "Marvelous! It will be nice to eat out—I haven't been away from the lodge in weeks." A sudden thought occurred to her and she put in hurriedly, "On the other hand, I've heard the new chef at The Crescent isn't very good. Maybe we'd fare better here."

She made a mental apology to the man she'd just maligned, but she couldn't chance running into Webb and Sheila on a cozy dinner date.

"I didn't plan on taking you to The Crescent," Tom said. "Don't worry about a thing—I'll make all the arrangements. All you have to do is be ready at four o'clock."

He hung up shortly after that. When Cristina replaced her own receiver, she cast a restless glance around the room. Since she had so much free time, she really should go on a housecleaning spree or something equally virtuous.

For fully a minute and a half, she tried to decide on a worthy project. Then she resolved to do great things another day and carried a mohair afghan to the big davenport in front of the fireplace. She stacked two cushions at one end and proceeded to make herself comfortable with a new novel. If the plot was good, she'd be able to forget her problems; if it was dull, she'd probably fall asleep and accomplish the same end.

When four o'clock came, she'd sampled both therapies and it was a considerably more cheerful young woman who answered the door to Tom's knock.

He took one look at her dark brown velvet dinner suit with a frothy lace-trimmed blouse and let out a long admiring whistle. "You look absolutely terrific!" he said in a wondering tone, still unable to stop staring. Then he recovered enough to grin and say, "If I'd known, I'd have been here an hour earlier."

"I was still drying my hair an hour ago," Cris said, happy that her efforts had apparently been so successful.

Tom's attention dutifully moved upward and he

noted how well the coppery shade of her hair went with the ivory lace blouse. His gaze lingered on the soft waves which framed her face before they disappeared into a neat French twist at the back. "If you ever show up at the lodge in jeans again," he announced finally, "I'll call a general strike."

Cris took a peek behind him and shivered. "I'll be more apt to appear in a raincoat. What on earth's happened to the weather? It looks as if we've gone straight from August to December." Her glance came back to doubtfully survey his lightweight sport coat. "Are you going to be warm enough?"

"I have an overcoat in the car. Need anything else?" he asked as she put a silk topcoat over her arm and picked up a small pouch handbag.

"I don't think so." As she followed him out, she caught a glimpse of a sleek gray sedan parked in front of the chalet. "That's Mr. Brock's car. What happened to yours?"

"William decided that you deserved something more fitting for a night out than my old wreck."

"Yours isn't a wreck—it just has character."

"And age," he said drily, helping her into the luxurious interior of the manager's car and then going around to slide behind the wheel.

Cris waited for him to leave the lodge parking lot and turn onto the main road leading down the mountain before leaning back and saying, "How did things go at work today? Anything more difficult than usual?"

"I didn't hear of anything. Actually I wasn't at my desk most of the day. You weren't the only one taking time off."

"Mr. Brock must have been in a good mood—to let two of us off the leash at the same time."

He grinned in response to her teasing but kept his attention on the two-lane road, which was slick after the day's rain showers. Overhead the gray storm clouds which hid the mountain were now misting the slopes of the lower peaks.

Cristina followed his glance and peered through the windshield. "It looks as if this could get pretty thick later on. Maybe we'd better not risk staying out for dinner." She sighed. "I certainly didn't think we'd have to worry about fog in August. Rain, maybe—but not fog."

Tom nodded. "Watch the cancellations roll in if this weather continues. It's a good thing Colby decided to do his hiking yesterday, although"—he gave her a quick sideways look—"you didn't do too well. What happened exactly? I thought you were familiar with that trail."

"I didn't watch where I was going." She half-turned in the seat to survey his profile. "Didn't Webb tell you?"

"He just said that you'd fallen on the trail and he thought you should see a doctor in case you'd cracked a rib. What was he doing while all this was going on?"

"I didn't notice at the exact minute," she said drily, "but about five seconds later, he was picking me up. I wouldn't have made it back to the lodge on my own," she added, trying to be fair.

"It doesn't sound as if he's quite the lounge lily that you thought."

The combination of rainy weather and Tom's curiosity made it hard for Cris to keep a cheerful attitude. She decided that she couldn't do anything about the rain, but she could change the subject. "What did you do with your free time today? Read a good book and take a nap the way I did?"

He shook his head. "The weather was still dry for most of the morning so I decided to get out and enjoy it. Now I'm glad I did."

"You mean you went hiking?"

His color deepened at her incredulous tone. "What's so strange about that?"

"Nothing at all. It's just that I didn't think you cared for it," she added apologetically. "You've never shown any interest before."

"Well, don't go buying me a rucksack for Christmas on the strength of it. I probably won't do it again for another six months. Certainly not unless the weather improves."

"I hope you didn't try the ice caves trail too."

"Not after I heard about your fiasco. I just wandered down that Reflection Lakes segment."

"How was the trail? I forgot to look at Kazy's report on it."

"What does Kazy have to do with it? I thought he was hired to be a gardener?"

"Now you're beginning to sound like Mr. Brock. What's wrong with a gardener taking a walk on his day off?"

"Is that what he did? Well, don't expect me to write trail reports in my free time," Tom said with some annoyance. "I spend half my life writing reports that nobody ever reads as it is. Most of them are so dull that I can't blame them."

Cristina nodded without commenting, since he seemed so vehement on the subject. The road had straightened as they reached lower altitudes and the general visibility improved, but rain continued to fall, settling to a monotonous drizzle. A half mile on, the lodge road merged with an arterial alongside a short landing strip where three private planes were parked on the runway. A sightseeing helicopter had already been pushed into a small hangar, and the ticket office had a "closed" sign in the window.

"Somebody else is taking the afternoon off," she said, gesturing toward the deserted airfield.

"They might as well." Tom checked the clock on the dashboard. "We're cutting it pretty fine on your hospital appointment. It's the last one on their schedule today—aside from emergencies." His expression lightened. "And looking the way you do now, you'll never fit in that category."

"How long are you going to be in town, sailor?" she asked with a smile.

"Long enough. What's come over you? If this is what a cracked rib does, I want to be with you on your next hike."

"It must have been the shock of getting a day off." She was unwilling to admit that having Webb under the same roof had challenged her to make a few changes, especially after he'd devastated her ego the night before. Tom's response to her latest efforts was encouraging, but she'd have to make sure he didn't get serious about their relationship.

She let the silence lengthen and Tom gave her a puzzled glance. "What's the matter? Are your ribs hurting?"

"Not much. It's probably the onset of starvation. I forgot to eat lunch today."

"I'll see about making a dinner reservation while you're in the hospital. The place we're going is new so it might be crowded."

"I didn't even know there was a new place in town," she confessed. "How did you hear about it?"

"Somebody at the lodge mentioned it," he said vaguely, slowing as they reached the outskirts of the village and turning off the main road where a sign said "Hospital Zone—Drive Slowly." A few minutes later he was braking in front of the emergency section of a one-story brick building which housed the hospital and professional offices as well.

The hospital had no difficulty attracting orthopedic specialists, as there was a preponderance of skiing patients during the winter months and young doctors soon discovered it was a good place to combine business with pleasure.

Tom walked with Cristina to the outpatients' door and then left to make their dinner reservation, promising to wait for her in the car until she was finished.

It didn't take long for her to be whisked through the up-to-the-minute X-ray department, and when she dressed again, she heard the happy news that she was practically as good as new. "Bruised but not broken" was the medical consensus. A young doctor also showed her how to care for the skin abrasions and finally offered some cheerful advice about staying off hiking trails for the next two weeks unless they were paved and level.

When Cristina was on her way back to the parking lot, she decided the dark brown velvet suit was an unqualified success; she'd had to remind the doctor twice to write a prescription for the lotion he'd suggested. A small smile played around her lips until she approached the car and saw Tom's stormy expression.

"Sorry—I didn't mean to keep you waiting," she told him. "It takes a while to fill out all the forms for the business office."

"You weren't long," he replied, helping her in and then ducking quickly back into the driver's seat so he'd be out of the drizzle. "Everything go okay?"

"Yes, thanks. 'Bruised but not broken' is the diagnosis," she said lightly. "It's nice to have it confirmed. Now I intend to consume your expensive dinner without a qualm—" She broke off as he grimaced. "What's wrong?"

"All the dinner reservations were taken. If we want to show up, they'll try to squeeze us in—but they aren't promising anything. Who the hell would think it in a place like this?"

"Who indeed?" she asked, determined to cheer him up. "Obviously they must have something we don't have at the lodge."

"A surplus of paying customers?"

Her lips twitched. "That, too. I was talking about an unusual chef. Either that or everybody just wants to go to the new place in town. Where is this magnificent new emporium?"

"A few blocks out on Crescent road," Tom said, making a left turn at the arterial and accelerating. He drove rapidly through the business section, which had been recently transformed by the merchants into what they fondly believed a Swiss mountain resort should resemble. Cristina surveyed the soggy display of steep-roofed buildings with their ornate wooden balconies and decided that it was just as well there weren't many Swiss visitors at that time of year.

When Tom pulled into a crowded parking lot a few minutes later and she saw a sign proclaiming "The Wagon Wheel" over a plain cement block building, she turned to stare at him. "Are you sure this is the place?" she asked. "Six months ago it was a feed store."

Tom shrugged and turned off the ignition after

taking the last parking space. "At least it's a logical transition—only the customers are different. We might as well give it a try. Apparently everybody else in town is here."

He was still muttering about the crowded parking lot as he followed her inside the restaurant building. They drew to a stop in a shadowy and slightly forbidding room with a bar on one side of it.

Tom narrowed his eyes as he tried to see through the gloom. "All the people who drove those cars in the parking lot must be someplace," he began just as an elderly woman dressed in a long print dress came through a door at the end of the room.

She hesitated and picked up a bucket of ice, before coming around the polished counter. "I'm sorry, we're not serving anything in here until later. You'll have to come back after the dinner hour."

"But dinner is what we wanted," Tom interrupted, looking confused. "My name is Warden—you were going to try and work us in."

"Oh, yes, Mr. Warden." The hostess pursed her lips. "I don't think there's a single place, but let's go through and check the reservation list to make sure." Seeing their puzzled looks, she smiled gently and beckoned for them to follow. "You came in the back door. If you don't mind walking through the kitchen—it will save some time."

"We'll be glad to," Cris said as Tom caught her elbow and followed practically on the hostess's heels. They went through a cool storage room with canned food stacked neatly on metal shelves and then into a brightly lit kitchen where three cooks were working behind a stainless steel counter and half a dozen waitresses were collecting orders. They were all so busy that no one even raised an eyebrow at finding customers behind the scenes. The hostess smiled over her shoulder again as she pushed open a swinging door and led them out into a crowded dining room unlike anything Cristina had ever seen.

The owners had duplicated the pioneer days custom of bringing covered wagons around the circle of a campfire. Diners were happily ensconced at tables in the canvas-covered prairie schooners while being served by women in long dresses and sunbonnets made from "flour sack" prints. A crackling fire burned in an open fire pit in the center of the room.

"No wonder everyone wants to eat here," Cristina said when the hostess finally pulled up at a high oak desk by the main entrance to the dining room and got out her reservation list. "The only things missing are the Indians and the cavalry."

"We try to make up for that with the food," the older woman said with a smile. "I'd like to accommodate you," she went on, "but there just isn't a single vacancy tonight. If you'd only called sooner," she admonished Tom, "we'd have done our best to serve you. I've eaten some wonderful meals up at your lodge."

"I told her that we were interested in seeing what our competition offered," Tom explained to Cris. Before she could reply, he turned again to the hostess. "Would you object if we joined some friends of ours?"

"Why, not at all. We can always squeeze in two more chairs without any trouble. Where are they?"

"Right over there at the end of the room." He was so pleased with his discovery that he didn't hear Cristina's sharp indrawn breath when she followed his gaze and identified Webb and Sheila. "I'll go over and ask if they mind," Tom announced and was off before she could stop him.

"Isn't it nice that everything worked out so well," the hostess said, picking up two menus and beckoning for Cristina to accompany her. Obviously she took it for granted that the merger was already accomplished.

Cristina wished she could ooze out of sight through the oak flooring. She had seen Webb's sudden frown when Tom first confronted him. The fact that Webb had then belatedly remembered his manners didn't alter her resolve. She was still mentally shuffling a sudden headache versus an onset of dizziness when she reached their table. Tom turned to greet her with a relieved smile.

"It's okay, Cris. Sheila says they'll be glad to share." He beamed down on the blonde woman who was wearing an elegant sheath of Thai silk. "You've saved our lives."

"You see, I am good for something," Sheila told Webb before she turned to greet Cristina. "Please sit down. There's plenty of room for four and we haven't even ordered yet."

"Thank you, that's very kind." Cristina hesitated and then reluctantly sat down in one of the chairs which a busboy had just brought. She took care to sit as far as possible from Webb, as she wondered whether anyone else noted that he hadn't bothered to acknowledge her presence with more than a nod. She listened to Tom explaining how they'd mistakenly come in the back door of the restaurant as she studied her menu, trying to look as if food were of paramount importance.

Evidently she didn't convince Webb. He simply

waited until Sheila and Tom were deep in a debate
on the merits of fried chicken versus pot roast before he folded his own menu and said, "Did you
have the X-rays before you came here?"

Cris emerged briefly from her printed protection.
"Yes, thanks."

"Well?" he said brusquely when the silence
lengthened.

Her eyebrows went up. "I beg your pardon?"

"So help me," he said in a pleasant conversational tone that didn't interfere with the discussion
at the other side of the table, "I'll take you back to
that hospital myself if I don't start getting some an-
swers in the next thirty seconds."

She glared at him. "All right, then—I'm fine.
Thank you." The last two words were tacked on reluctantly.

His sudden grin showed that he knew it. "You'll
be better after some dinner. I promise you," he
said, and signaled to the hovering waitress that
they were ready to order.

By the time Cristina was halfway through the
first course, she knew the real reason for the restaurant's success. Whoever reigned supreme in the
kitchen at the Wagon Wheel was a real marvel.
The soup was a good indication; it was served
piping hot from an old-fashioned tureen and was
thick with vegetables in a subtly flavored but
hearty beef stock. Tiny herb dumplings bobbed on
top to add the final savory touch.

Afterward the waitress brought a heaping platter
of fried chicken accompanied by baking powder
biscuits that were light and flaky. Containers of
amber fireweed honey were placed alongside.
Mashed potatoes and country gravy were served
family style, plus fresh garden peas swimming in

butter. When it was time for dessert, the pleasant, middle-aged woman offered wild blackberry pie still warm from the oven.

Cristina wasn't surprised that most conversation stopped when the first course was served. After that, there was only a few crucial decisions such as who deserved the last piece of chicken and whether to risk a third biscuit just before the pie arrived.

Sheila appeared as captivated by the food as everyone else. "I have no intention of leaving a thing," she had told Webb almost defiantly when the first course appeared. "Probably I'll be dieting for the rest of the month to make up for it."

"That's ridiculous," he replied; "your vital statistics don't matter a damn with people who love you."

Cristina kept her own gaze on the other diners in the room as she thought about Webb's comment. It had been offered in an offhand, almost brotherly manner, she decided. Either that, or his relationship with the woman at his side was secure enough that it wasn't necessary for him to bother with social pleasantries. She found that thought so depressing that it was a relief to concentrate on food to the exclusion of all else.

Later Tom expressed the general sentiments at the table when he finished his dessert and said over his coffee, "If I ate any more, I'd have to be carried out the door."

"I may have to be, anyhow," Sheila said. "Does anyone have a cigarette? I've finished all mine." She turned to Webb before he could respond. "And don't tell me that I'm smoking too much—"

"I wouldn't think of it," he replied mildly. "I'll see if I can buy a pack for you."

"There's no need." Tom leaned forward, offering his package across the table. He waited for Sheila to take one, saw Webb and Cristina shake their heads, and selected one himself before putting it back in his shirt pocket. "You know," he went on thoughtfully as he reached for his lighter, "I've figured out the solution to all our lodge money problems. If we could serve food like this, the customers would come no matter what the weather."

"You'd be picketed by the Weight Watchers within a week," Sheila told him.

"Make that two days," Cris said with a faint smile. "I'm going home and throw my recipes in the fireplace."

Webb looked amused. "You're all missing the point. We'd better see if we can't buy stock in this place."

"That would solve your problem," Tom agreed.

"I don't have a problem," Webb corrected him. "Don't forget, I'm just a guest at the lodge. Not even a paying one at the moment, unless Cristina presents me with a bill at the door when I leave."

"That's Tom's department," Cristina told him, determined to match his nonchalance. "Right now we're in your debt for allowing us to share your table. I hope we didn't interrupt anything."

Sheila's shapely lips twisted. "Hardly. Webb was probably glad to see some cheerful faces. Things didn't turn out the way we'd hoped today." For a moment, there was a bleak look in her eyes until she made a determined effort to dispel it, saying, "Maybe I should sue my astrologer."

Webb reached across to cover her hand on the top of the table. "I've told you everything will be

all right," he said in a gentle tone that Cristina had
never heard him use before. "There'll be other
days. It's just a matter of time."

The solicitude was so pronounced that even Tom
must have felt the vibrations. Cristina let out a sigh
of relief as he reached for his wallet to pay part of
the check and then pushed back his chair, saying,
"We'll have to get back to the lodge. Our manager
doesn't believe in the accountant having a whole
day off. Only assistant managers like Cristina
here."

Webb's brows came together even as he got to
his feet and helped Cris on with her coat. "You
both had the day off?"

From his voice, it was obvious that he thought
they'd spent the time together. She saw no reason
to correct him. "Why, yes. I understand you had
something to do with it," she went on blandly. "It
certainly pays to have influence at court." She
tucked her hand under Tom's arm and felt a moment of satisfaction as she saw Webb's scowl
deepen.

Tom had been busy bidding good-bye to Sheila
and missed the interchange. All he said when he
shook hands with Webb was, "I presume you have
a car to get back to the lodge?"

"That's right," Webb replied as he let his gaze
linger on Cristina; "but I may be late arriving at
the chalet."

"Heavens, you don't have to make any explanations to me," she told him lightly and smiled at the
woman by his side. "Good night, Sheila. I hope I
see you again."

It was hardly a sparkling farewell, but it was the
best Cris could think of just then. She did manage

to cling devotedly to Tom until they were safely through the restaurant door. As she waited at the entrance for him to bring the car around so that she wouldn't have to go out in the rain, she leaned dispiritedly against the step railing.

Webb couldn't have been more explicit in showing his affection for Sheila if he'd taken out an ad in the newspaper. Even so, the blonde woman's words during dinner had intimated that there was something keeping them apart. Probably her husband, Cristina thought with some bitterness, hoping the missing Mr. Simmons wouldn't give up too easily. Surprisingly enough, her rancor against Sheila had dissolved in the last hour. It was easy to understand how any woman, married or not, would respond to a man like Webb Colby.

Cris could testify to that—even supply the chapter and verse of when it happened to her.

She'd been aware of his impact when he'd strolled into the lodge that first morning. By the time he'd moved to the chalet, her emotions had come alive with a vengeance. The episode in the loft had provided the final touch, awakening a desire she hadn't known she possessed. Now she had to face the fact that for Webb it had simply been the passionate aftermath of a difficult day—an interval of physical satisfaction as far as he was concerned, but nothing more.

The future appeared to offer the same dismal prospects. When Cristina thought of the empty days ahead it caused an ache in her chest far more painful than any of her visible ailments.

At that moment, Tom's headlights swept the entrance and he pulled up in front of the door. Cristina straightened and even managed to smile as she crossed through the downpour to the car. At least she wouldn't have to make any excuses for her wet cheeks; Tom would simply blame them on the weather. Unfortunately, she knew better.

Chapter Seven

◆◆◆◆◆◆◆◆◆◆◆◆◆◆◆◆◆◆◆◆◆◆◆◆

It was just after midnight when the telephone rang at the chalet. Cristina discovered the time when she turned on the bed lamp and fumbled to find her slippers. Then, as the slippers proved elusive and the phone kept ringing, she muttered an exasperated "Damn!" and started for the stairs without them. On the way down, she realized that she hadn't bothered with a robe either. That thought brought only a moment's hesitation as she realized that Webb would have answered the phone on the first ring if he'd returned to the chalet. She was still mulling over that depressing thought as she reached the living room and picked up the receiver.

"Miss Kelly?" It was the lodge operator. "I have a call for Mr. Colby. Would you put him on, please."

"I'm sorry, Mr. Colby isn't here." Cris brushed a strand of hair back from her cheek as she sank into the chair beside the telephone table. She had just started to say that she'd take a message when she heard a noise in the hallway behind her.

Turning, she almost let the receiver slip through her fingers as she saw Webb, clad only in a white terrycloth robe, emerge from the bathroom and come to a startled halt.

With one swift movement, he shouldered the towel he was carrying and cinched up the belt on his robe before asking, "What in the hell are you doing up?"

His appearance confused her completely, making her forget that her own costume was hardly conventional. Her pale pink nightgown was long-sleeved, with a demure embroidered collar, but the thin fabric faithfully recorded every curve underneath.

Webb's masculine glance swept over her, not missing an inch on the way. His only visible reaction was to frown more deeply and add, "Are you all right?"

"Of course, I'm all right." Her words came out automatically.

"Well, in that case—can't it wait until morning?" He gestured to the receiver dangling from her grasp.

She blinked and stared down at the beige phone, as if observing a strange new appendage. Then she pulled her mind back into a functioning unit. "It isn't for me," she snapped.

"Wrong number?"

"Not at all." Two could play at that game, she decided, and waved the receiver carelessly before putting it on the table. "This time it's for you."

He started toward it and then pulled up. "Find out who it is."

Cristina's impulse to argue died aborning as she saw his authoritative expression. She put the receiver to her ear again. "This is Miss Kelly. Are you still there?" There was an instant's pause as she listened to the operator and then she said, "I'm sorry to keep you waiting. Mr. Colby just came in. Could I tell him who's calling, please?" There was another pause. Then Cristina's lips thinned, "I see. Just a moment." She turned and offered the receiver to Webb. "Mrs. Simmons."

"Thanks very much," he said, taking it. He clamped a hand over the mouthpiece as he added, "You'd better put something else on or push up the heat. You shouldn't get chilled on top of everything else." After that, he turned his back on her and spoke into the mouthpiece. "Hello, Sheila, what can I do for you?"

Cristina, who was scurrying up the stairs, noted the difference in his tone and wished that, just once, she could inspire the same reaction, but she didn't wait to hear more. When she reached the loft, she put on a matching velour robe and went over to retrieve her scuffs from under the edge of the bed. It only took another minute to run a comb through her hair and use her lipstick. As she stared into her oval mirror, she realized that it would be simpler to go back to bed; there was no need to trudge downstairs and reopen hostilities.

Having reached that sensible conclusion, she took a final look in the mirror and promptly headed for the stairway.

Webb's phone conversation made her pause halfway down. "I was beginning to think you'd never get there, Charles. What in the devil kept you so long? I almost ran out of delaying tactics in the meantime."

Cristina saw a grin come over Webb's face as he listened to the mysterious Charles's answer. Then his amused expression faded and was replaced with a look of concern. "When did all this happen?" he asked. A minute later, he said thoughtfully, "And it's been raining ever since. Damn! That could mean trouble. Well, we can't do any-

thing now until morning." The look of amusement
returned to his face. "There's no use expecting you
for the early shift, I suppose. I didn't think so.
Okay, give me a call when you're back in circula-
tion. If I'm not here, I'll leave a message with the
switchboard operator at the lodge." He waited a
moment and then said, "That's all right, Charles—
forget it. You can buy me a drink sometime. See
you tomorrow then. G'night."

His last words made Cristina hurriedly move
down the rest of the stairway, and Webb turned to
observe her as he put down the receiver.

Once she reached the bottom, she hesitated, unsure of her next move. Then she decided that hun-
ger was always a legitimate excuse, whatever the
hour, and started toward the kitchen.

For once, it appeared that she'd done the right
thing as far as Webb was concerned. He followed
in leisurely fashion and watched her open the refrigerator door before he said, "Something hot to
drink sounds good to me. How are you at making cocoa?"

"About the best you'll find at this time of night."
She looked over her shoulder at him. "Might I suggest that you get rid of that wet towel and put a
few more clothes on."

A slow grin creased his face. "Hoist with my
own petard, eh? Okay, but I'll be back. Incidentally, I like my cocoa made with milk."

"You're lucky—so do I," she said, getting out a
kettle and putting it on the stove. "This won't take
long."

Webb was back by the time she poured the
cocoa into two mugs on the counter. He had
changed into dark blue pajamas with a tartan wool
robe over them. Coming over to the counter, he

picked up his mug and took an appreciative sip of its steaming contents. "This tastes good." His glance went over her changed appearance as if he'd just noticed it. "Pink on a redhead—but damned if it doesn't look great. Even better than that velvet outfit you had on earlier."

His compliment was so unexpected that Cris choked on her cocoa. "I'm not a redhead," she got out finally when he promptly took the mug from her grasp and whacked her on the back.

"You're close enough." He watched her retrieve her property with some enjoyment and then followed her in to the davenport. "I'm sorry about that phone call waking you up. I was in the shower or I'd have answered it."

"So I gathered." She took another swallow of cocoa and cradled the mug between her palms. "It doesn't matter. I'm glad you appeared when you did, though. I hadn't realized you were here."

"That's understandable. I suppose you heard me talking to Charles later . . ." Webb said, looking at her thoughtfully over his mug.

She was quick to catch the resigned tone of his voice. "I couldn't help it, but you don't have to explain anything."

"Amazing. Such forbearance," he goaded her gently. "Hardly a feminine trait."

"But then I've been associating with you for the past two days and I've learned so much," she told him sweetly. "It's a case of necessity, since I never know whether you'll be in the mood to drink cocoa or threatening to pitch me over the bannister. That's why I'm not asking questions now."

He sighed. "I can't blame you—considering that you already have your quota of bruises this week.

Maybe an apology would be in order. On my part, of course."

"Of course," she agreed serenely. "But right now I'd settle for a small explanation instead. Who in the dickens is Charles?"

Webb's grin flashed. "That's more like it," he teased, but when he saw her brows go up dangerously, he relented. "Relax, Cris. Charles is my best friend and incidentally . . ."

Her eyes didn't waver. "Incidentally what?"

"He's married to Sheila. Very much so—no matter what else you thought." Webb sighed as he leaned back against the cushion. "Like most married couples, they hit a snag not long ago. Sheila got tired of staying home and wanted to go on with her modeling career. Charles could see her point of view, but his work keeps him in this type of country while hers had to center in California or New York. The only solution was for one or the other to commute whenever they could snatch a weekend. Hardly a satisfactory arrangement."

Cristina nodded. "One of those situations where there isn't a good compromise."

"Exactly. Naturally there were some hot words exchanged in the course of things, and it took a little doing to get them both here on neutral ground."

She started to smile. "How did you work it?"

"It wasn't hard. I needed Charles's help on a project—and besides that, I had their dog."

Her features lit up as she remembered. "Of course—Tessa!"

"Tessa, indeed. Never underestimate an Irish setter on a mediation board. Besides, once the atmosphere cooled, I knew that they'd be falling all over each other again."

"It didn't look as if Sheila was anticipating a reconciliation with her husband when I saw her at the restaurant tonight," Cris observed. "I thought she was pretty happy to have you by her side."

Webb's jaw jutted stubbornly. "I was afraid you'd see the situation that way. You're as bad as she is for leaping to the wrong conclusion."

As Cris remained pointedly silent he raked his fingers through his hair and shifted on the couch to face her more squarely. "I suspected that you'd have to hear the whole story before you were convinced. Actually, Charles promised to meet us earlier in the day. When he didn't arrive, naturally Sheila thought the worst."

"I'm not surprised."

Webb made a derisive grunt, but he didn't try to defend his point. Instead he went on. "Charles has now arrived at The Crescent and the long-awaited reconciliation is going very nicely."

"I'm glad," Cris said sincerely.

"So am I," he said with undeniable emphasis. "That wasn't what he called to tell me, however. Did you authorize any work up on Myrtle Creek today—above the falls?"

"Why, no." Her brows drew together. "There's a maintenance crew which checks the stream beds to make sure there aren't any obstructions. We do that in the late fall when there's a threat of flooding. Not at this time of year—" She broke off at the sound of wind and rain gusting against the kitchen window, positive evidence that the storm was still continuing outside. "Of course, Mr. Brock could have heard a weather report this week and decided not to take any chances. That stream has caused trouble in the past."

"What kind of trouble?"

"It overflowed and washed away an acre of topsoil in the meadow two seasons ago. That's why we
have that netting down now." She chewed absently
on her lower lip. "You don't think one rainstorm
like this could cause trouble?"

"I would doubt it." Webb got up and reached
for her empty cocoa mug. "We can go look in the
morning. There's no point in discussing it now." He
yawned hugely, as he walked into the kitchen.
"Lord, I'm tired. It'll be nice to get some sleep for
a change . . ." His voice dropped as if he suddenly realized what he'd said, and he turned on
the water in the sink, making a project of rinsing
the empty mugs.

Cris shot a quick look at his engrossed figure,
thankful that he couldn't see her own flaming
cheeks just then. Apparently she wasn't the only
one to feel the effects of that kiss the night before.

She kept her voice carefully casual. "The cocoa
should help your cause along tonight. I'm going on
up to bed now. See you in the morning."

By the time Webb turned around, she was at the
top of the spiral stairs, and a moment later, the
light in the loft was clicked off. He lingered in the
kitchen, frowning thoughtfully up at the darkened
area. Then his jaw tightened and he headed for his
own bedroom. There was no mistaking the sound
when he closed the door sharply behind him.

Up in the loft, Cristina heard the noise and
shifted restlessly on her mattress. As she stared into
the darkness, her wistful expression was more revealing than she knew.

It was still raining when she awoke the next
morning and stared unbelievingly at her bedside
alarm. Eight-thirty! She made a soft sound of disbelief as she picked up the clock and listened, be-

fore turning it over to check the setting. Then she said "Damn!" in a tone that had nothing soft about it. Naturally the alarm didn't function if the button wasn't pulled out. William Brock would be fit to be tied when he learned she'd overslept again. She pulled on her robe and just stopped to run a comb through her hair before hurrying down the stairs.

The two cocoa mugs were still on the kitchen counter from the night before, but there was no sign of anything new in the way of breakfast. Cristina hurriedly filled the percolator with water and spooned in coffee before plugging it in. Then she went over to Webb's closed bedroom door and knocked briskly.

When there was no answer, she opened it a crack and peered inside only to discover that her prize guest had vanished again. She frowned slightly at the empty but still rumpled bed. The fact that Webb hadn't bothered to straighten the covers as he'd done before showed that he'd been in a hurry to leave the chalet. She cast another look around the room, hoping that he might have left a scribbled note for her, but that was an exercise in futility, too. Cris frittered away a few more minutes making his bed, without stopping to analyze what compelled her to do it. When she finished, she gave the nearest pillow an extra little pat and headed for her shower.

It was a half hour later when she got around to donning her rain jacket for the walk across to the lodge. The bark that Kazy had strewn so carefully on the flower beds earlier in the week looked dull and soggy after the hours of steady rain. Cris let her gaze wander over the parking lot and wasn't surprised to see that the crop of campers and vacation trailers had thinned since the weather change.

Apparently she wasn't the only one who was disenchanted by the disappearance of summer.

Webb's comment about the problems of Myrtle Creek made her hesitate before turning toward the lodge entrance; then she shrugged and pushed on through the doorway. She was late to work already and had no excuse for hiking over the countryside without first consulting Mr. Brock.

She soon found that it wasn't going to be easy. There was a crowd of people around the cashier's window intent on checking out. The regular clerk was hopelessly swamped and Cristina moved over quickly to assist her, signaling for Yoshi to come from behind the reception desk as well.

It was twenty minutes later before the exodus was over and Yoshi was able to say wryly, "We won't have any trouble accommodating Mr. Colby in the lodge now if he wants to move back from your place." She broke off to answer the telephone and hung up a moment later to add, "Another cancellation—that's the fifth this morning. All because of this miserable weather."

"I know." Cris picked up her jacket from the chair where she'd tossed it when she'd first come in and put it on a hook by the mail counter. As she passed the manager's office, she saw that his door was open but his familiar figure was missing. "Where's Mr. Brock?" she asked Yoshi, when she got back to the desk. "Or should I even ask?"

"If he'd stayed around, he'd probably be committing hara-kiri by now. But he had other things to worry about earlier."

Cristina reached up to cover her ears. "I'm afraid to ask. Has anything gone wrong with the repair work in the annex?"

"Oh, no." Yoshi shook her head. "That's going according to schedule. The painters should finish this afternoon."

"Don't tell me that Jimmy overslept and we're short of bellboys again."

"Hardly. The day that Mr. Brock starts carrying suitcases you'll need a padded truck to take him away." Yoshi's smile flashed. "Nothing so drastic as that—he went out with Kazy to see how the repair on the lakes trail is coming along. He was afraid that this rain might have caused even more damage up there." She broke off at Cris's perplexed expression. "I forgot that you weren't around yesterday. That's what happens when you have a day off."

"For a minute, I thought the padded truck would have another passenger," Cris said, with relief in her voice. "What's wrong with that trail?"

"Some idiots tried a shortcut on the last switchback above Reflection Lake and ruined about six feet of the barrier at the edge of the path. With all this rain, a hiker could take a nasty tumble. Mr. Brock was worried about the lodge's liability when Kazy and I told him about it. He was so impressed with our report that he put Kazy in charge of the trail repair."

"I see." Cris kept her voice casual as she said, "Then Webb . . . I mean . . . Mr. Colby didn't go with them."

Yoshi pursed her lips as she tried to remember. "Not that I noticed. He was closeted with Mr. Brock this morning before the dining room opened, and then I got busy on the desk so I don't know where he went after that." She leaned eagerly over the counter. "Why? Didn't he tell you where he was going?"

"There was no reason why he should." Cristina

didn't volunteer that she'd already searched the
chalet for a note. When she observed Yoshi's avid
expression, she decided it was time to change the
subject. "Has the weather caused any other problems with the trails?"

"Not that I've heard—but there really isn't anybody around to ask. The guests that aren't checking out haven't been very sociable. One of them
had breakfast and then told me he was going back
to bed for the rest of the day."

"We could schedule a bingo game in the lobby
this afternoon and put out some jigsaw puzzles to
help things along."

"I'll update the bulletin board," Yoshi said, jot-
ting it down. "Where are the puzzles?"

"Tom said I could store them in his office cabi-
net. I'll ask him for the key."

"Don't bother hurrying." Yoshi's comment caught
Cris before she'd taken more than a step or two.
"He isn't in his office yet. That must have been
quite a dinner date that you had."

"It was very nice but we were back early," Cris
confessed. "There's no way I can blame oversleep-
ing on my social life. I just plain forgot to set my
alarm. If anybody comes looking for me in the next
fifteen minutes, I'll be in the kitchen going over
menus with the chef."

"Which translates to . . ."

"Having a cup of coffee. Raise the flag if you
need me."

When she returned a quarter-hour later, Yoshi
said there was nothing worth reporting except that
two more parties had checked out.

"I'm glad I didn't have an omelette along with
my coffee," Cris said wryly. "Obviously we can't
afford it."

Yoshi shuffled her housekeeping records into a neat pile. "I'm going out and pray for sunshine on my coffee break. If the weather gets any worse, I'll be unemployed by next week."

Cristina grinned at her. "Things aren't that bad." Then she added thoughtfully, "Going out sounds like a good idea, though. Certainly better than staying here and watching our guests disappear."

"The repair crew should be about finished on the lakes trail by now," Yoshi offered.

"It wouldn't hurt to take a look." Cristina reached for her jacket and put it on. "In case I miss seeing Mr. Brock, I'll be back in an hour or so. Any messages for Kazy?"

"None that won't wait until lunchtime," Yoshi said. "Just make sure that he doesn't fall down the mountainside. I have plans for him."

Cris nodded cheerfully and headed for the lodge entrance, pulling up her jacket hood as she went. The lobby windows showed the rain was still falling but she was practically rainproofed with a nylon windbreaker over slacks and sturdy shoes.

She walked across the parking lot and cut up to the meadow and the start of the lodge trail system. That main path was the fastest access to the others, branching off for the Reflection Lakes sector just before it came to Myrtle Falls.

As her eyes went over the soggy turf, her steps slowed and finally stopped. If two days of rain had left this meadow with water almost standing on it, Webb's cryptic question about Myrtle Creek took on added importance. Evidently Charles Simmons had reported something to arouse his suspicions.

A worried line appeared on Cris's forehead as she walked on along the path. If there had been any real damage in that section, someone would have reported it to the lodge by now, she reasoned. Mr. Brock wouldn't be on the lakes trail if help were needed somewhere else.

She was still trying to convince herself when she came to the fork on the path. She had told Yoshi that she was going to Reflection Lake, but there was little she could do to assist Kazy and his crew at this point. If Myrtle Creek overflowed its banks, the consequences could be a real disaster.

Cristina tightened the strings on her hood to keep it over her hair and started hiking briskly along the left-hand trail.

She had only taken a few steps when she heard her name called, and she turned to see Tom loping up the path from the lodge to join her.

"I just missed you," he said, still breathing hard when he came alongside. "It's a good thing I wasn't farther behind—Yoshi said you were headed for the lakes trail."

"I planned to," Cris said, wiping her wet cheeks with the back of her hand, "but I decided to visit the Myrtle Creek sector instead. Mr. Brock will have everything under control at the lakes, and this steady rain bothers me."

Carefully securing the visor on his nylon ski cap, Tom checked the solid gray overcast above them. Even the mighty mountain was completely shrouded in thick, dark clouds. He pulled the zipper of his own waterproof jacket up tight against his chin. "It bothers everybody. I don't see why we can't be bothered in comfort while we're drinking coffee at the lodge."

Cristina's eyebrows went up in amusement. "This isn't a command performance. I thought coming along was your idea."

"Well, everybody seemed to be taking to the

hills. I thought I might be missing something at the lodge."

"You are," she told him wryly. "You're missing being trampled by a steady line of guests checking out early. I couldn't bear to stay around and watch."

Tom looked almost as pained as Yoshi when he heard the stark truth. "As bad as that, eh? When you combine a rainy weekend with the additional expenses from the fire in the annex . . ."

Cristina raised her hands in despair. "Don't say any more—I have a perfectly good imagination of my own."

"Sorry, I forgot that you've more at stake than your salary." He looked around at the rain-soaked landscape. "Why don't we go back to the lodge and sit in front of a nice warm fire? Myrtle Falls will keep until another day."

Cris considered his earnest face thoughtfully. No matter how he tried, he looked out of place as soon as he stepped from behind his desk. His disciplined, sometimes pedantic manner fitted with ledger books and double-entry bookkeeping, and she suspected that he kept his emotions strictly in balance, as well.

"Well, what do you say?" he prompted impatiently.

"About going back, you mean?" She shook her head. "I'd rather not. I'm already as wet as I'll get, and the fresh air feels good. But there's no need for you to come along. Two days in a row of outdoor life is a little drastic for you," she teased.

"I'll manage," he said resignedly, motioning for her to start walking. "Frankly, though, I think this 'back to nature' routine is overrated."

She lengthened her stride to match his as long as

.e path would permit two of them abreast. "I can see why you were disappointed with the lakes trail yesterday. It should be back to normal by now though."

He shrugged. "A few potholes more or less. Nothing to make a fuss about."

Cristina thought he was taking it remarkably calmly considering the lodge's liability if a guest was injured—until she remembered he was an accountant, not an insurance broker. She kept that in mind as she decided not to mention the problems that might be facing them in the Myrtle Creek sector. Instead she strode along in silence beside him, content to enjoy the quiet, almost muted aura that the misty weather put on the spectacular scenery. The steep icy slopes of Rainier were somewhere there in front of them, leading almost straight up to heaven. Or at least ten thousand more feet on the way, Cris thought as she tried to discern the rough outlines of the peak and failed completely. There was only the fog which hung like a silver curtain at the edge of the valley. She could still see part of the ice caves trail as it wound into the first switchbacks. A few sturdy evergreens stood in cleared pockets along it, their green branches shiny with moisture. There wouldn't be any more problems with dust on that trail until the sun reappeared and dried it out. Instead, hikers would have to cope with mud and slick rocks as they trudged up the steep stretches that day—another new challenge which contributed to the fascination of the wilderness.

"You're looking awfully pleased about something," Tom said, pulling out a handkerchief to mop his face. "Anything worth knowing?"

"Not really." She knew that Tom wouldn't be

particularly sympathetic to an environmental discussion just then. "Do you think the rain is letting up a little?"

"Not that I can see." He slowed his stride as the path became steeper, and the sound of Myrtle Creek became audible in the quiet morning air.

The stream which led directly down from a glacier on the mountain's south side was a force to be reckoned with at all seasons of the year. Just then, to Cristina's apprehensive ears, the water rushing over the rocky bed sounded like the mighty Columbia. She swallowed over an obstruction in her throat that felt as large as one of the boulders edging the trail and quickened her pace, causing Tom to frown slightly as he had to hurry to keep up with her.

And then suddenly they reached the boundary of the stream, where it coursed through the misted meadow before starting down the hillside and erupting as Myrtle Falls.

Cristina pulled up, breathing hard after the climb. She clutched her chilled hands in front of her, trying to steady them as sudden relief poured over her.

All the fears she'd imagined were groundless. Myrtle Creek still was safely within its banks. It was deeper, admittedly, and brushing against the roots of some trees edging the stream bed, but still manageable. And, surrounding it, the soil of the alpine meadow was still intact.

Cris started to relax against a boulder at the side of the path when her glance caught some movement in the mist further along the creek. "What in the dickens is that?" she whispered to Tom, with a new sense of foreboding.

His eyes narrowed as he tried to identify the figures. "Can't tell from here. There are two of them"—he shifted his stance, attempting to determine the action—"and they're dragging something. What the hell . . ."

Cristina got up with sudden determination. "I think we'd better find out what's going on. I'm glad you're along."

"Don't worry," he said, taking her arm protectively. "It's probably just a couple of weekenders hoping to requisition our nursery stock where there's nobody to see."

"I hope you're right. People who steal evergreen shrubs aren't usually violent types."

Tom was squinting ahead of them as they walked along the sodden trail. "There's been a change in the plant world," he said grimly. "Make that tree trunks instead."

Cristina was almost having to run to keep up with his determined strides. "I didn't know there were any fallen trees here. Maybe there's been a washout, after all."

"We'll soon see." He raised his voice then, shouting at the two who were shifting a pile of branches at the fast-flowing creek's edge. "Hey, you there! What in the devil do you think you're doing?"

Cris winced at his belligerent tone, wondering what they'd do if the two men adopted similar tactics. Tom was more suited to verbal onslaughts than planting a right cross to somebody's jaw. She bent down, trying to locate a piece of wood as a cudgel, and thereby missed seeing the two men straighten in surprise. The first premonition of disaster came when she heard Tom's muttered, "Good god—wouldn't you know!"

"What's the matter?" she asked before she raised up and found out.

Webb Colby was standing motionless, staring back at them, his expression less than welcoming. By his side, a tall, fair-haired man wearing a plaid mackinaw and worn jeans appeared oblivious to the rain streaming down on his bare head.

Cristina's first inclination was to simply turn around and disappear in the mist. Since Tom's steps were considerably slower than before, she suspected he was having similar qualms.

Webb finally took the initiative when they got within ten feet. "Do you still expect an answer to that question?" he asked Tom in a carefully level tone.

Cristina decided that he had an unfair advantage and immediately went to Tom's defense. "Maybe he doesn't—but I'd like one." She gestured toward the fallen saplings at their feet. "Somebody should have told you that there isn't any cutting allowed in this area. We're having enough trouble keeping our ground cover as it is. Lord knows what damage those trees could cause if they interfered with the stream flow."

The tall man beside Webb cut in when she stopped to catch her breath. "Don't shoot, lady. We're not guilty." He put his hands in his pockets and smiled in a way that made his long, thin face undeniably attractive. "You must be Cristina—Sheila mentioned a green-eyed copperknob around these parts."

"You mean that you're . . ." Cris swallowed as words failed her.

"Charles Simmons," Webb supplied in a tone of voice that still sounded icy. "Cris Kelly and our accountant, Tom Warden."

"I've met your wife, Mr. Simmons," Tom said, shaking hands with him. "Cris and I had dinner with her last night."

"So she said." From Charles's imperturbable tone, they might have been holding court at the Ritz rather than beside an alpine stream-bank in the rain. "I'm sorry that I wasn't there."

"Charles couldn't join us because he was busy working on a project for me," Webb emphasized. He looked solid and formidable in a hip-length green waterproofed jacket worn over jeans which were rain-darkened below the knees. A worn ski cap was pulled squarely down over his forehead. "Charles is a forestry expert. He works on higher yields these days—not the other way around."

"We weren't accusing you with making off with the silver," Cris said evenly. "Actually we hadn't even recognized you when Tom shouted."

Charles's pleasant features didn't alter. "That's a relief. Those trees were already cut when we came along, but for a minute I thought you were going to shoot first and explain later."

"I'm sure you were trembling in your boots," Cristina said, responding to his smile. She let her glance go over his tall frame before she gestured toward the cut saplings on the bank. "It doesn't matter so much about this wood—although it would be a good idea to haul it away from the stream bed." Then her smiled faded as she looked across to Webb. "I presume this wasn't the project you were talking about."

Charles spoke up gently before Webb could answer. "That's right, Cristina. He just wanted my opinion on a parcel of lodge-owned timberland. You know, yield possibilities and all that."

Webb was watching her expression. "Go ahead

and tell her the rest of it, Charles," he said, bridging the awkward silence following the forestry man's words. "She might as well have the bad news now as hear it later. I *did* plan to show you a copy of the final report," he added when Cris's apprehensive expression changed to a mutinous one.

"How kind of you. Some people would even have told me what was going on long before this," she said in a silky tone. At her side, Tom cleared his throat uneasily, clearly wishing that he was miles away as Cris continued with her questioning. "Exactly what is this news that you have to relate, Mr. Simmons? I gather that it isn't good."

Charles's expression showed that he didn't welcome having to spell it out. "It isn't a cause for celebrating," he began slowly. "According to my calculations, cashing in on your timber resources could only serve as a stopgap measure. You'd be far better off financially to sell the land for development—if you can still get the amount that Webb said you were offered."

"Sell the property!" Cristina's eyes widened in disbelief. "Why, I hadn't even thought of such a thing." She whirled to face Webb. "And you have no right to be commissioning a report like this."

"I don't, but my mother does. It's time you faced facts, Cristina." His tone was as annoyed as hers.

"Webb, there's no need to be so hard on the girl," Charles protested.

"Do you think I'm enjoying this?" Webb's expression was still bleak, but he attempted to soften his words as he turned back to her. "It's unfortunate that your grandfather left the final decision with my family. All I'm trying to do is find the best solution for the resort before you lose your shirt."

His mouth quirked up at one corner. "Figuratively speaking, of course."

"Of course." There was no hiding the bitterness in her voice. "And your mother will follow your recommendation—is that it?" When he hesitated, she said, "Just answer yes or no. I think you at least owe me that."

Tom put a hand on her arm. "Take it easy, Cris—there are bound to be some alternatives."

"He's right," Webb confirmed. "I'm certainly not going to decide the fate of the lodge standing here in a downpour this morning."

"*Will* your mother follow your recommendation," Cris persisted, her figure taut with anger.

He took a deep breath as if trying to hang on to his temper. "Obviously she will. Why in the hell do you think I came up here in the first place?"

"That's all I wanted to know," Cristina said. Without another word, she turned and headed back down the trail toward the lodge.

Tom caught up with her as she reached the edge of the meadow. "Cris, for lord's sake—what's got into you? There's no reason why you can't discuss things with Colby calmly and logically."

"You stay and discuss things." She bit out the words without slackening her stride. "I hope I never see him again."

"That's a ridiculous thing to say. Did you forget that he's living with you? Well, not exactly living with you," he apologized as she shot him a furious look, "but it's hard to ignore somebody under the same roof."

"He can have the roof. There's plenty of room for me in the lodge until he goes back to California."

"What good will that do? Be sensible, Cris.

There's nothing to be gained by alienating the man at this point. Actually he's doing you a favor by suggesting that you sell—or haven't you looked at the financial side of this operation lately?"

Cristina's steps slowed reluctantly as she gave him an unhappy glance. "We were starting to get into the black. Mr. Brock even said that this summer could be the turnaround. Besides, there's more to the lodge than just dollars and cents. I thought you'd understand." Her voice was husky with emotion.

"I do, Cris, honestly." Tom reached over then and pulled her tightly against him. He didn't try to further the embrace, simply holding her protectively until she finally relaxed. Then he brushed his lips over her wet cheeks and released her. "Let's continue this when we have a roof over our heads." He shot an annoyed glance heavenward. "Otherwise we'll drown before we get off this damned trail."

Cristina gave a smothered choke of laughter. Tom was right—it was hard to remain intense about anything with rain dripping off one's nose and chin.

He caught her hand and pulled her close beside him again as they started down the path. "When you're warm and have some hot coffee inside you, the idea of selling out won't sound so bad either," he commented. "Probably your grandfather would be the first to agree with Colby's decision."

Cristina pulled her hand away under the guise of getting a handkerchief from her pocket but forebore arguing with him. There was no use; he was simply trying to appease her outrage after learning of Webb's deceit.

Tom ignored her silence as he went on. "Simmons was right. The price that development company offered was nothing to sneeze at—" He broke off when Cris wrinkled her nose and suddenly did just that.

It was enough to make both of them laugh. Afterward, Tom exhibited more tact than usual by dropping the subject for the rest of their hike to the lodge.

It was the middle of the day when he caught up with her again, this time checking work schedules in the housekeeping department. He drew her aside for a minute to ask, "Were you serious about planning to stay here in the lodge overnight?"

"I certainly was. Why? There are plenty of rooms, so there's no problem, is there?"

"Not that I know of," he admitted, "but there's no point unless you want some company. I just overheard Yoshi taking a message for our dear manager from Colby. He sent his regards and said he was sorry not to see him before he left."

Cristina felt an instant's elation which changed quickly to an inexplicable feeling of loss. "Where was Webb going?"

"San Francisco, according to Yoshi. He was leaving the chalet right away and asked her to convey his thanks for your hospitality." Tom tacked the last on almost reluctantly. "Guess he knew it was a good time to leave."

"Did he say if he was coming back?" Cris knew that her question was far from casual, but just then she didn't care.

Tom stared at her as if he couldn't believe his ears. "Why in hell should he come back?" he began loudly and subsided with an effort. "After all, he accomplished all he planned to. Possibly in more ways than one." At Cristina's puzzled look, he added, "I'd like to know why Sheila was sticking so close to him. Maybe he just hired Charles Simmons to make sure he was out of the way."

"That could be." Cris kept her tone level, but she felt an inward twinge of revulsion at Tom's accusation.

"Anyhow, I thought you'd like to know that it was safe to go back home in case you were staying away for a reason." His glance took in her damp and wrinkled slacks. "The rain's letting up, too. Maybe that's a good sign."

At that moment, Cris would have swallowed a potion made from bat's wings and lizard's feet if it would have changed her luck. "Let's hope so," she said wearily. "I'll pray to the rain god and the weather bureau when I go to change my clothes." She smiled at him. "I believe in hedging my bets."

A little later as she hurried along the path to the chalet, she was happy to see that Tom's weather forecast still held. There was a dull, leaden look to the sky, but the rain had stopped and the gentle breeze had shifted to the north, usually a sign that promised fair weather.

When she came around the corner of the chalet, however, she discovered the immediate forecast still held some turbulence as far as she was concerned. Webb was putting his luggage in the car, and if he was enchanted by her sudden appearance, he hid his delight very well.

"The grapevine's faster than usual today," he commented, slamming the car door and walking back to the porch steps to retrieve his topcoat and attaché case. "I thought I'd be off the premises before you appeared." He watched her wary approach with some amusement.

She stuck her hands in her pockets, trying to

hide her apprehension. "Tom said you were on your way to California."

"Tom does get around," he said. "Did he also mention that I was coming back?" As her figure stiffened, he added wryly, "I gather that he didn't. If all goes as planned with plane connections, I hope to be back here tomorrow afternoon." He shot a glance at his watch. "We'll have to talk then—there isn't time now. I'm cutting it fine as it is."

"Don't let me stop you." Her words came out with difficulty.

Webb stared at her slim figure on the bottom step of the porch. Her chin was set at a defiant angle; her face looked pale and unhappy. There was hostility in her shadowed green eyes, but shock was mirrored there too, as if she was still trying to recover from what he'd said earlier. "Listen, Cris—do me a favor. Don't go leaping to conclusions. There's a lot about this that you don't know."

"That's more than evident," she said, trying to keep her voice from trembling. "I hope you'll tell me before the bill of sale goes through."

"Oh, hell! There's no use talking." His angry gaze raked over her in a way that made her step back hurriedly.

"If you lay a hand on me, I'll ... I'll ..."

"Relax, honey." He gave a disgusted snort. "Laying a hand on you is the last thing I'd do right now."

A sudden silence fell between them, as they both remembered another leavetaking that had involved considerably more parts of their anatomy.

The color that flared in Cristina's cheeks as a result didn't go unnoticed. Webb's stern expression softened as he said, "If you need help while I'm away, contact Charles. He and Sheila will be staying at the lodge. Please trust me in this, Cris," he added quietly. He stood there a moment longer, as if imprinting her features on his memory before he got in the car and drove away without looking back.

She stared numbly after him until the station wagon disappeared around the curve on the main road. Then she clasped her hands tightly together and climbed the porch steps.

Feminine instinct told her that if she'd made the slightest response in that last minute, the leavetaking would have been far different. Which was exactly why she hadn't made the slightest move or response, she told herself.

As she went on into the chalet and closed the door behind her, she had time to reflect that among her other newly discovered faults, she was fast becoming a congenital liar.

Chapter Eight

◆◆◆◆◆◆◆◆◆◆◆◆◆◆◆◆◆◆◆◆◆◆◆◆◆◆◆◆

A phone call from Sheila caught Cris at the reception desk later that afternoon.

"You're a hard woman to find," the blonde said
cheerfully over the wire. "The operator told me
just to hang on while she rang the various nooks
and crannies. Did you know that Charles and I are
now official guests at the lodge?"

"Webb mentioned it—" Cris started to say, only
to have the other interrupt.

"Oh, you *did* see him then. I'm so glad. He told
Charles that he hoped to explain a few things before he left."

"As far as I'm concerned, there's a great deal still
to explain," Cris said, trying to sound as if it didn't
matter.

Sheila must have sensed that she was on thin ice.
"That makes two of us—I haven't a clue about
what's going on either. Charles just quotes that old
saying, 'Explanations usually deceive one party or
the other and usually both,' when he wants to shut
me up. I don't know why I'm dithering on about
it—the real reason I called was to invite you to join
us for dinner."

"Tonight?"

"Uh-huh. In about an hour if that's convenient. I

hope you don't mind invitations on short notice. Charles just got in or I'd have called earlier."

It was impossible to mistake the friendliness in Sheila's voice and Cris found herself responding, despite the fact that the Simmons were in the enemy camp. "I really should change—" she started to say, only to have the other interrupt again.

"That's all right. You can join us at our table whenever you're ready. Just a second . . ." There was a murmur of conversation in the background and then Sheila came back on the wire. "Charles says there's a dance later on and insists that you join us." She gave a gurgle of laughter. "He intends to catch up on his social life in a hurry."

"Well, if you're sure I won't be interfering—I'd love to join you. Actually I promised Mr. Brock that I'd be at the dance. He's given me so much time off recently that I felt I should work late."

"Good! You can enjoy yourself and feel virtuous at the same time. We'll meet you in the dining room in about an hour. Oh, before I hang up—what should I wear?"

"At our dances, anything between jeans and ostrich plumes looks just fine."

Sheila giggled in response. "Then my long-sleeved jersey should be all right. Persuading Charles into a shirt and tie might be more difficult. It's a good thing he's in a mellow mood at the moment."

When Cristina hung up, she took a minute to mull over Sheila's last comment. The way things sounded, the Simmons were very much back together and pleased about it, as well. So much for Tom's suspicions about Webb and Sheila. It was amazing how relieved she felt at that conclusion and she was still in a cheerful frame of mind when

she went over to change clothes at the chalet. The
prospect of eating with the Simmons was immeasurably better than sitting alone in a corner of
the dining room before going on to supervise activity on the dance floor.

Under those ordinary circumstances, she would
have probably put on the handiest thing in the
closet. This time she selected an emerald green
Pierrot blouse with its flattering ruffled collar and
cuffs, plus a flared skirt in the same shade.

She was glad of her choice when she walked into
the dining room a little later and saw Charles get
to his feet at a table near the fireplace.

"This is my lucky night," he told her as he held
her chair and then sat down again. "From the looks
of things, I've cornered the two prettiest women in
the place. It's a pity that there are laws against po-
lygamy in this country," he commented to Sheila
on his other side.

"You'd better believe it," his wife told him amia-
bly. She smiled at Cris and said, "We'd just about
decided on the roast beef. Does that sound good to
you?"

"Fine, thanks. I don't think we can match the atmosphere of the restaurant last night," Cris replied
when the waitress had taken their order, "but the
chef here is very good and roast beef is his
specialty."

"It sounds great to me after cooking over a
campfire for the last few days," Charles said. "De-
hydrated beef stew loses its appeal fast—among
other things."

The quick glance he gave his wife showed that
he wasn't referring exclusively to trail fare and her
soft flush indicated she was well aware of it. For

an instant, Cris felt awkward, eavesdropping on their personal affairs.

Charles must have sensed her discomfort, for he turned back to her promptly and said, "I was sorry that you and Webb had that misunderstanding this morning. Unfortunately you got away before he had a chance to explain."

"So he said." Cristina sat back so that a shrimp cocktail could be put in front of her. "It really doesn't matter."

Sheila broke in determinedly. "Why discuss business now? After all, this is a kind of celebration for Charles and me."

"You're right, darling." He reached across the table to clasp her hand. "Take a lesson from us, Cristina," he added lightly. "When you get married, don't let stubborn pride force you into things that you really don't want to do at all. At least Sheila and I were lucky—Webb was around to pound a little sense into both of us. Not that he hasn't had his own problems."

Cris tried to think of a noncommittal answer to that and decided to stay silent when she couldn't come up with one. Just then, she had no desire to hear a discourse on Webb's previous emotional involvements. Whoever the unfortunate women were, they undoubtedly lost the most. There was nothing in Webb's assured manner now to indicate that he'd suffered in past dealings with the feminine sex.

She was just on the point of mentioning it to Charles when Tom came threading through the tables toward them. He was dressed more formally than usual, in a blue oxford-cloth shirt with a striped tie under a well-fitting tweed jacket, and

Cris found herself responding to his enthusiastic greeting.

"Yoshi told me that you were working the dance," he said, after saluting Sheila and shaking hands with Charles. "When I heard that, I decided to put in a little overtime myself. You don't mind if I hang around when the dance starts, I hope."

"Of course not," Sheila beamed at him. "It's just the thing to put Charles in his place. I think he's been having fantasies of collecting a harem ever since Cristina sat down."

"Well, it was nice while it lasted," her husband told her. "Have you had dinner?" he asked Tom. "We can get another chair for you to join us."

Another was being rounded up by an obliging busboy even as he spoke, and Tom subsided into it, saying, "I'll just have some coffee while you eat. Bill Brock and I had dinner earlier in his office—going over the accounts."

"That can't be good for your digestion," Sheila said.

"Not this month," Tom agreed. He caught Cristina's unhappy look and added hastily, "We'll work something out. We always do."

"Of course you will," Charles concurred a little too heartily. "I hadn't realized that this was such a great place for a vacation."

"In your type of work, I'd think this kind of a weekend would be strictly a busman's holiday," Tom told him.

The other man acknowledged it. "Usually Sheila and I head for palm trees and sandy beaches when we get some time off. Maybe we've been missing something, though. I suppose you and Cristina are experts in this terrain."

"That's being generous," Cris put in wryly, thinking that Webb obviously hadn't told him about her clumsiness en route to the ice caves. "Actually I haven't done much hiking this season, and Tom was out for the first time yesterday. He was investigating the lakes trail on his day off."

"That's one I haven't heard about," Sheila said, perking up. "Is it difficult?"

"Nothing to it," Tom told her. "Strictly for the wife and kiddies."

"There's a part under repair at the moment," Cristina put in, "so I wouldn't recommend it."

Tom shrugged aside her caution. "A few potholes—nothing more."

"Well, you should know," Charles agreed, his voice solemn. "I had other plans for my time off, but if that's what my wife would like to do—"

"We can talk it over later," Sheila interrupted hastily. "Right now, let's finish dinner. The dance must already have started because I can hear the music."

"There's no rush," Cristina said, helping her to change the subject. Charles's scarcely veiled amusement showed exactly how he intended to spend his time off, and his wife's reply did nothing to quench his enjoyment. "The combo is made up of two bellboys and a waiter," Cris went on, giving Sheila a chance to recover. "They're enthusiastic musicians, so the dance is the high point of their week. Isn't that right, Tom?"

"It must be," he agreed. "They even forget to charge for their overtime." He took a swallow of coffee. "Actually, they're pretty good."

Charles looked thoughtful. "Do you both attend the dances each week—on a working basis, I mean?"

"Lord, no. Cris and I usually have better things

to do." Tom pulled at his ear, obviously trying to remember how long it had been. Then as he saw Cristina's slight frown, he realized how his comment must have sounded. "Not that we aren't looking forward to it tonight," he put in hastily. "Good company makes all the difference." He broke off as the others started to laugh. "Oh, hell! You know what I mean."

"Tom and I don't have much time off together," Cris explained to the other two when the laughter subsided. "When we do, we usually go for a drive or down to The Crescent—just to see different surroundings."

"Like last night," Sheila supplied. "It was too bad that you left that restaurant early. Somebody turned on a jukebox, so Webb and I took a turn around the floor. He's a marvelous dancer. What a pity he couldn't be here tonight."

Cris almost announced that the only way she'd share a dance floor with Webb Colby would be from opposite sides of the room. Since that was hardly diplomatic, she concentrated on buttering a roll while the conversation went on to other things.

She wasn't able to avoid mention of Webb completely, however. Charles came stubbornly back to him later at the dance when the two of them were conveniently isolated in a corner of the lobby floor.

"I wish Webb was still around to thresh things out," he began abruptly as the combo segued into a fox trot and they were assured of another interval of music. "I know that he planned to explain things later on, but I don't think that's quite fair to you." Charles put up an admonishing hand when she started to interrupt. "Hear me out. Webb didn't fly back to San Francisco just to get his mother's approval on selling, no matter what you think."

"Well, that's certainly the impression he gave—"

"Maybe that was deliberate, too," Charles cut in. "He wants to make sure you don't rock the boat while he's gone. There've been too many 'accidents' here to be coincidental. Surely you realize that. No—keep on dancing," he ordered when she pulled up in astonishment; "this may be the only chance I'll have to talk to you alone."

She let herself be pulled back into his arms, aware that they had moved close to the big lobby windows while the main body of dancers was circling decorously in front of a makeshift bandstand. "I wondered how so many terrible things could happen in such a short time," she said in a low voice, "but there was never any reason for us to be suspicious. Certainly no tangible proof. Do you think Webb might have uncovered something new?"

"Possibly enough to try running down leads, but no actual evidence that would stand up in court. They're too clever for that."

"Who's 'they'?" she asked, startled.

"The people who'd stand to make the most if you sold the property."

"After your report on the timber, I suppose that means the development company." She wrinkled her forehead as she tried to think. "It's just a firm in northern California. I've never met any of the principals."

"Not officially," Charles granted. "Unless they put someone here to help their cause along." At her puzzled response, he went on to explain, "Right now you haven't any clues how that fire started in the annex the other night. It could have been accidentally caused by a guest, I suppose."

"Probably one who checked out the next day."

Charles nodded. "Or it might have been an employee who's still around. I can tell you this—it wasn't any leprechaun who put those trees across Myrtle Creek to try and dam the flow."

"So that's why the two of you were checking up there this morning," Cristina said, her voice rising. "You cleared them out and that's what you called Webb about last night."

The musicians led up to the final chorus of the music and Charles started to dance her back to the center of the floor. "Don't start using your imagination at this point," he cautioned. "Webb doesn't want you to get in trouble. He'd give me hell if he knew I was even talking to you."

Her eyes widened in surprise. "You make him sound like the Lord High Executioner and the Chief Justice rolled into one. Surely his opinion doesn't count for that much!"

Charles let out a chuckle. "As chief spokesman for the Mathews' family interests around the world, he doesn't even have to raise his voice. I respect his opinions, and he's been a friend of Sheila's and mine for years. Long before he served as best man at our wedding."

"I see." Cristina bit her lip, a little chagrined at Charles's sturdy defense.

"But I don't blame you for getting the wrong impression," Charles acknowledged. "Webb's as stubborn as they come—and he was worse than usual today." As the music stopped, he hesitated before leading her back to their chairs by the fireplace. "Usually he's completely unflappable, but after that encounter with you by the stream, he lost his temper completely. Just like all the rest of us in our weaker moments." Charles grinned down at her. "I think if you'd stayed around much longer, he'd have thrown you in the middle of Myrtle Creek."

Cris tried to hide her embarrassment. "I'm sorry to be such a disrupting influence," she began, only to have him cut her off.

"I'm not—it's the best thing in the world for Webb. Both Sheila and I are waiting around to see what happens."

"Well, if you hear an explosion tomorrow when he gets back, you'll know where to look for your suspect," Cris said, as he put a hand under her elbow and guided her off the floor.

"I'll remember. But if Webb unearths the information he wants in California, I don't think you'll have to worry about any explosions. On his part, anyway. Later on, you'll find that a reconciliation has all sorts of advantages. Isn't that right, my love?" The last was said to Sheila as they joined the others.

Tom stood up before she could answer and put his arm around Cristina's waist to lead her back onto the floor. "Come on, Cris—I have a feeling that we're too young to hear any more. Now's the time for you to teach me how to rhumba."

She followed him obediently but said a minute later, "It would be easier if they weren't playing a cha-cha-cha."

Tom shrugged and looked around. "Then let's go sample that punch bowl in the corner until they play something else." He observed a young couple performing what appeared to be an Apache rain dance on the edge of the floor. "Might as well do calisthenics as that," he noted in some disgust. "And don't give me that old routine about dancing to a different drummer."

Cris giggled and filled a punch cup for him.

"You've mangled the quotation but I know what you mean. Ummm, this is good," she said, taking a sip after she'd filled another cup. "No wonder the attendance is so good at these affairs. The recipe for fruit punch has changed since I went to dancing school."

Tom took a taste. "The bartender picked the wrong bottle when he reached for the orange juice. Or the right one," he said, taking another appreciative swallow. "What did you and Charles find to talk about for so long?"

"The usual." Cris kept her tone noncommittal. "He was telling about Webb's working for the Mathews' family concerns."

"That's one way of putting it. From what I read, Colby makes all the decisions now since his stepfather retired three or four years ago. The old fellow still attends the board meetings, but that's all. I'm surprised Webb could find time to come up here and look over the lodge. This property is pretty small potatoes compared to what he's used to."

"That may be, but he's not going to have things all his way," Cris said, stung by Tom's easy acceptance of the property disposal. "I can't think his mother would completely ignore other people's wishes. She knows how much my grandfather loved every inch of this land."

"You have to move with the times, Cris. Don't be too disappointed if Mrs. Mathews chooses to be practical in the long run."

"I'm certainly not going to give up without trying. Webb isn't the only one who can talk to her. I'll go down myself next week if I have to. If that doesn't work, I can always hire a lawyer to stop the proceedings, and you know how crowded court calendars are. Webb will find it isn't going to be as easy as he thinks."

"Well, don't let it spoil your evening," Tom replied. "You might as well take things as they come—and right now the music sounds like something I can dance to. Either that or this punch has taken care of my two left feet."

Cristina replaced her partially emptied cup on the table and followed him back to the floor. "If people circulate around that punch bowl much longer, the musicians can go home early and nobody will even miss them. Jimmy Bolton hasn't been working in the bar lately, has he?"

"Not officially." Tom swung her into a fast fox trot. "Why?"

"I don't know. Things just seem to turn out differently when he's around. If he keeps on the way he's going, Mr. Brock will either make him a vice president or he'll be out on his ear before the season ends." She glanced up to see an uneasy look pass over Tom's face. "What's wrong? I didn't step on your foot, did I?"

"After that punch, all my extremities are numb," he assured her. "Can't feel a thing."

"Well, something was wrong . . ."

"If you must know," he said, loosening his clasp so he could speak to her more easily, "it was your reference to dear old Brock that gave me a twinge. I wouldn't count on him for any long-range plans here at the lodge—but, for god's sake, don't let on that I said so."

They were alongside the windows, and Cristina pulled out of his arms deliberately so that she could get off the dance floor. "You mean that Mr. Brock is planning to quit?"

"You can't really blame him, Cris. Rumors get

around in a place like this, and if it's going to be the last season for the lodge, a man has to make plans."

"I see."

Tom's glance noted her pale face and the unhappy set of her chin. "Don't take it so hard, honey. There are lots of managers available if you can change Colby's mind about selling. Or maybe the development firm will find some way to keep the lodge in their future plans."

His well-meaning words simply made the cloak of despair settle even more solidly around Cristina's shoulders. For an instant she was tempted to flare back at him. Then she realized she could hardly expect him or Mr. Brock to feel the way she did about the lodge. To them, the resort was a job—not an integral part of their past or future. She was the only one who tried to put sentiment on a balance sheet.

"Hey, we'd better get back to the Simmons," Tom said, nudging her. "They'll think we've deserted them completely. S'pose they'd like some punch?"

"Let's go ask. They may not have tried it yet. As a matter of fact," she said, leading the way, "I think I'll have another cup, too."

"It sure helps on the dance floor," Tom assured her. He steered her around a couple as they walked over to where Charles and Sheila waited. "Drink enough of it and you'll end up with 'no sense—no feeling.'"

"Tonight," Cristina murmured, "it sounds like exactly what I need."

Chapter Nine

•••••••••••••••••••••••••••••••••••••

Cristina woke with a start the next morning. She frowned at the stream of pale light edging the curtains and managed to focus on the alarm clock. Only six-thirty—there was another hour before she had to get up.

She had just leaned back to burrow in the pillow when she heard the sharp ring of the telephone from down below.

"Oh, no—" she murmured, sitting up again and reaching for her robe. Nothing good was ever heralded by a telephone call at six-thirty in the morning. Unless it was a long distance call, she thought suddenly as she slid into her scuffs. She made a dash for the stairway, her unbelted robe streaming out behind her, and picked up the receiver as it rang again. "Hello . . ." she said, trying not to sound as breathless as she felt.

"Cris? Is that you?"

It wasn't the masculine voice she expected, and she sagged against the edge of the telephone table. "Yes, Tom. What's gone wrong now?"

"Hey, what's the matter with you?" He sounded inordinately cheerful. "Too much punch last night?"

Cristina's fingers tightened on the receiver. She wished she could simply replace it and go back to

149

bed. "I feel fine, thanks—considering what time it
is."

"Oh, that!"

"And considering it was after two o'clock before
the dance broke up," she went on. "Unless the
world's coming to an end, call me back in an hour
or so."

"Wait a minute. Don't hang up," he commanded.
"I've had the operator ringing you for the last ten
minutes."

"You mean the world *is* coming to an end?"

"I mean I should have pounded on your door instead of phoning."

"Only if you were carrying a cup of coffee in the
other hand." She decided she might as well wake
up because the prospect of going back to bed
didn't look feasible. "Sorry, Tom—what was it you
wanted?"

"It's not what *I* want," he said, sounding churl-
ish. "The park rangers called to say that the rain-
fall we had has played havoc with the ice caves
area. The ceiling on one of the caves at Five-Mile
Creek collapsed yesterday afternoon. They're closing some trails and thought we'd better do the
same until conditions improve."

Cristina frowned and chewed on her bottom lip.
"We'll certainly have to send someone up to inves-
tigate our sector. Who does Mr. Brock suggest?"

"You're talking to him," Tom said smugly. "Apparently our maintenance crew is still needed on
the lakes trail. You and I are the only two extra
'bodies.' Actually, I offered to go alone—but
William thought that you'd had more experience,
so he wants you to come along. I can be ready to
leave in twenty minutes."

"Well, I can't." She brushed a strand of hair from

her face and tried to see the kitchen clock. "I have to go over accounts this morning—otherwise the paychecks will be late this week. That will take two hours at least. You go ahead and I'll try to meet you later."

"I have a better idea. What about meeting me at the main fork when you're finished? I'll go up there now and erect a notice saying the ice caves trail is temporarily closed—so that the hikers will be discouraged and the lodge protected."

"That makes sense. You'd better get an extra sign at the carpenter shop in case we have to post one at the entrance to the caves, too."

"Okay. Anything else?"

"Not that I can think of right now. I'll bring along a thermos of coffee. It still looks chilly out, but I don't think we'll get rained on."

"I hope not." Tom didn't sound enchanted by the prospect ahead of them. "Too bad that our friend Colby isn't still around. He could jog up to the cave and be back before breakfast from the way Simmons talked."

"Webb didn't move any faster than most people," Cristina replied, knowing that he would have been amused to hear her defense.

Apparently Tom was, too. "I didn't think I'd get any disagreement from you," he said in some surprise. "The way you talked yesterday, he was two steps behind Simon Legree in your estimation."

"Let's not argue. At this hour even locating the coffeepot is a major project for me." She could have added that a six-mile hike up a steep, slippery path was another topic she'd rather not contemplate.

"Brock probably forgot that you're still in the 'walking wounded' category after your last trip up that trail," Tom said, as if he'd just remembered himself. "I don't see why I can't go alone."

"It's easier if there are two people," she said, not wanting to hurt his feelings. Aside from the past two days, she was sure he hadn't ventured farther than the parking lot all summer.

"We could invite Charles and Sheila to go along . . ." he said tentatively.

"I doubt if they'd be interested. This is supposed to be their second honeymoon. After four hours on that trail, there'd be more apt to be a homicide."

"Now she tells me."

She laughed. "You don't have to worry—you're bigger than I am."

"That makes me feel better. I'll see you about nine at the fork. You might as well work on those accounts at your place in comfort. The furnace thermostat is temperamental this morning, and it's colder than hell here at the lodge."

"That's all we needed to keep the customers happy," she groaned.

"Don't worry about it. On a gray morning like this, they're still snug in their beds. The heat should be up to normal in a little while. Go have your coffee and get to work. The sooner we get started up that trail, the sooner we'll be back," he said and rang off.

Cris was able to view the prospect with a little more enthusiasm when nine o'clock finally arrived. By then, she'd had a hot shower and breakfast followed by two cups of coffee to dispel any lingering sleepiness. Checking accounts had been time-consuming, but it was much pleasanter checking them in the nice warm kitchen than in a chilly room at the lodge. It was just fortunate that she'd remembered to bring them with her the night before when Tom had escorted her home from the dance. They also had helped avoid a lengthy leavetaking on the chalet porch. Trying to embrace a woman who was carrying an armful of account ledgers had its problems. Cris had simply smiled and said good night while Tom was still figuring how to accomplish it.

It hadn't occurred to her until then that Tom might be serious about their relationship, but his proprietorial manner at the dance made her realize that she'd have to find a way to discourage him without losing his friendship.

It was a pity that love didn't come to order. She had thought about that in the last few days. She'd also learned that it was no use denying the intense physical awareness that could occur between a man and a woman—call it chemistry or propinquity or whatever. She had danced in Tom's arms all evening long and felt nothing at all, while just the thought of Webb Colby a thousand miles away could make every nerve ending in her body start clamoring like the main fire alarm bell at the lodge.

Fortunately, it was one alarm that Webb wouldn't hear about. If she had any sense, she'd manage to work up a fine healthy hate that would salvage her pride if not her inheritance while he was around. In the meantime, she would concentrate on Tom's finer points and enjoy a day in the fresh air.

She kept that in mind as she put on wool slacks, stout hiking shoes, and her nylon waterproof jacket over a warm sweater. Her hair was tucked up under a ski cap and after another glance at the overcast sky, she pulled down the flaps to keep her ears warm. A vacuum flask of hot coffee, two concentrated fruit bars, and waterproof gloves were stuffed in a small knapsack which she carried easily over one shoulder. Before setting out from the chalet, she added a light folding shovel just in case Tom forgot to bring one along. This time she was taking no chances. And the ironic part was that Webb wasn't around to appreciate her efforts.

She spared another moment on the path to the lodge wondering if he really would be back by late afternoon or if that was more wishful thinking on her part. Although why she was eager to hear his bad news about the resort property was another irony. "A real masochist—that's me," she murmured as she went through the lodge doors.

A young bellman who was running a carpet sweeper over the rug inside looked up and said, "I beg your pardon, Miss Kelly?"

It was embarrassing to be found talking to herself, but since there wasn't another soul within fifty feet she couldn't pretend. "Pay no attention to me," she told him. "That's what happens if you stay in the hotel business long enough."

"Then it's a good thing I'm just part-time help," he replied, grinning.

"Do me a favor and forget about it. Oh—one more thing," she said as he nodded and started sweeping again. "Would you put these account ledgers on Mr. Brock's desk, please. I'm a little late."

"Sure thing, Miss Kelly."

Cris watched him go with an amused look and noticed that Yoshi was on the phone behind the reception desk. She waved at her but didn't linger because the lobby clock showed that she was already fifteen minutes late and there was still a ten-minute walk before she could reach the fork in the trail.

When she did get there, she found Tom sitting

on an uncomfortable-looking boulder with a small wooden signpost propped up beside him. She saw that he'd already erected another sign at the beginning of the ice caves trail nearby, warning that the area was temporarily closed to hikers.

"Has it had any effect?" Cris asked, sitting down on a rock to catch her breath.

"It discouraged three women, but they didn't look very enthusiastic to start with," he replied, lighting a cigarette.

"Sort of like us," she said, wishing that she could turn back to enjoy the blazing fire that she'd seen in the lobby fireplace. There wasn't any wind to contend with, but the sun still lurked behind an overcast and the day felt more like late November than August. It looked more like it, too, Cris decided, and shivered despite her thick sweater.

Tom closed the zipper of his down jacket after replacing his lighter in his shirt pocket. "We should be warm enough once we get moving. I was beginning to think you weren't coming at all."

"I'm sorry. I couldn't get organized." Why was it, she wondered as she apologized, that he looked as if he'd donned a costume for the day. His jacket was more suited to the Arctic Circle than the northwest and offered no protection if it should rain. Then she remembered her decision to use positive thought as far as he was concerned instead of making comparisons. "Being a little late is the story of my life," she confessed. "At least the account ledgers were delivered on schedule."

"I'd wait lots longer than a half hour for you," he said then with an earnestness that was almost embarrassing. Fortunately, he went on to change the subject immediately. "Why do we need two shovels for putting up one sign?" He gestured toward the one she was holding.

"A good question," she said. "We don't." She looked around, trying to find a place where she could leave hers and retrieve it on the return journey. "I'll tuck it back in the underbrush out of sight," she said, suiting her action to the words. When she returned, Tom had hoisted the wooden sign to his back, carrying it easily in a rope harness. "That's a slick arrangement," she approved. "Want me to tuck your shovel back there, too, so your hands will be free?"

"Okay," he agreed, giving it to her. "I didn't think I could persuade you to carry it. What's in your knapsack?"

"Coffee and some calories in case we get hungry." She pushed the small shovel tightly against the signpost so that it couldn't work loose and tested the result. "I think we're ready now."

"You're sure you feel up to this?" Tom's solicitude rang slightly false because he had already turned onto the trail, leaving her to follow in his footsteps.

"I'm fine, thanks," she said, wondering if he planned to follow the 'mighty hunter' routine for the entire hike. At least she wouldn't have to make polite conversation that way, which was some compensation.

Tom set a good pace on the first mile of the trail, where there was very little change in elevation. He was the kind of hiker who kept his eyes strictly on the ground ahead of him, not even commenting on a noisy jay which circled directly overhead. Cris slowed for an instant to follow the bird's flight and cast an involuntary glance up the bare hillside to their left where the sociable marmot had whistled that other time. Today he was probably nestled in a warmer spot, waiting for the sun to come out. Which showed that he had more sense than some humans, Cris decided as she blew on her palms to try and warm them.

Tom finally pulled up to rest when they crossed the stream where Webb had bathed her ribs on the other trip. Cris kept her eyes averted from the bank, wishing that all those memories didn't keep flooding back with such heartrending emphasis.

Tom must have been watching her face. "What's the matter? We haven't even started on the steep part yet." He indicated the section of trail ahead of them.

"I know," she said, trying to hide her annoyance. "Let's go on, shall we? We'll need a rest period more later on."

"Okay—whatever you say. I don't know what the rush is, though. Looks to me as if we'll have the whole place to ourselves. The weather must have discouraged everybody." He surveyed the vacant landscape around them with satisfaction. "I sort of like this solitude."

"Right now, I'd trade it for a little bit of sunshine." She glanced at the clouds above the ridge leading to the glacier. "I think that overcast is thinning though. Maybe things will improve for our return trip."

"Maybe." He eased the rope harness on his shoulders and looked up the steep trail. "Want to lead the way?"

Which was a nice way of salving his masculine ego, she decided, smiling as they started off. For a few feet, she set a fast pace and then slowed as common sense prevailed. Both of them would need all their stamina on the steep muddy trail still to come.

It was considerably later before they reached the edge of the moraine at the top of the ridge. Cris could scarcely believe that conditions had changed so much within days. The soil which had bathed her in dust before had become as slick as black ice where it coated the rocks on the stream bed, and resembled a spongy bog in the pockets where rainwater still stood.

"To think people do this for fun," Tom complained as he paused to scrape some mud from his boot sole onto a rock. "My god, they must be out of their minds!"

"It's different when the trail's in better condition. You should know that from your hike to the lakes the other day," Cris said, still breathing hard from the last steep switchback. "Although that route wasn't in the best of shape, was it?"

"I don't remember," Tom was still trying to dislodge a stubborn particle. "It's not my job to act like a park ranger in my free time."

Cristina decided that he must have gone down the lakes trail with his eyes half-closed that trip, but she didn't mention it. He was in a bad enough humor as it was. She said instead, "I'm starved. Shall we find a good spot and drink our coffee?"

"I don't care about coffee, but I'd like to sit down for ten minutes. Don't any of these rocks have a flat side?"

"Certainly not," she told him as they walked past where she and Webb had eaten their picnic lunch. "That's a specialty of this trail. Anybody can have flat rocks—we advertise pointed ones."

"Ummm." Tom clearly wasn't amused. "How

about up on the moraine at that signpost where the trail forks again. What are we advertising there?"

"The two different routes to the ice caves. You can follow that stream"—she pointed to a ribbon of gray water meandering through the plateau—"or cut up over the ridge beyond. The ridge is faster but it takes more energy."

"Let's decide after we have the coffee," he said, and silence settled between them until they came to the sign at the fork of the trail.

Cristina shrugged her knapsack from her shoulder and put it on the ground at the base of the post. Then she turned and watched Tom slip out of his harness, dropping the rope, shovel, and signpost none too gently in a pile on the ground. She chose to ignore that and said cheerfully, "You have your choice of a mountain view"—she gestured toward the mist-shrouded flanks of Rainer—"or would you prefer the Tatoosh Range in the fog?"

"Who cares?" Tom sat down, facing the mountain, wincing as he came into contact with a sharp rock in the process. He extracted it from under his hip and tossed it away. "I don't care much for the upholstery in this diner."

She shrugged with true *maître d'* insouciance. "*Monsieur* can always go to another establishment."

He grinned reluctantly. "Okay—you win. I just hope the coffee's hot."

"So do I," she said, pouring it. As she handed him a steaming cup, she added reflectively, "I can't decide where I need this most—inside or outside. Unfortunately, it would take ten minutes to unlace my shoes and find out if my toes are frozen, so it's hardly worth it."

"You could always try pouring it over your

ankles. That's where my blood settled after the last climb," Tom grumbled. He was staring out across the bleak acres of rock in front of him. "You know, this place looks like one of those moon craters in a science fiction film. Talk about being desolate!"

Cris nodded. "It's not as depressing when there's sunlight and blue sky. Usually there are other people around, too. That helps."

"So does this coffee," Tom said, taking a deep swallow. "How about something to go with it?"

She fished in the knapsack and tossed him a foil-wrapped bar. "Concentrated fruit and nuts— that should help, too. One of the few things that's nutritious and still tastes good."

He watched her extract another bar for herself and smiled in relief. "For a minute, I thought I'd have to divide this one," he said, unwrapping it and taking a satisfied bite. "One thing about hiking—it gives you an appetite."

"Among other things," Cris said, wishing that some warmth would come back into her toes.

"What's the story on these ice caves?" Tom sounded more like his normal self when he finished his fruit bar and hunched forward to drink his coffee.

Cris frowned slightly. "What do you mean?"

"Well, I know that they're caves, but why are they here?"

"The summer temperature is behind it," she said, cradling her warm coffee mug between her palms. "That causes the melt water and eventually a stream which runs under the ice. In time, it causes a tunnel and then even more air flows into it. That warm air increases the melting and, after a while, an ice cave results. This recent rain would saturate the snow at the end of the tunnels so there could be cave-ins at any time for the next week or so. It's similar to avalanche danger on the snow fields."

"What good can we do with one little sign?"

"We only have one cave in this sector that's deep enough to be a real danger. The last I heard, it went back about three hundred feet. Unfortunately, that's plenty of room for a hiker to get into trouble."

She took a final swallow of coffee and shook the last few drops onto the ground before packing the mug back in her knapsack. Tom did the same and handed his over as well.

"I gather you and Webb didn't get this far the other day," he commented.

She smiled wryly. "Nope. I fell over a rock back down the trail a ways and he had to shepherd me back to the lodge."

"So the man can't be all bad. Now that you've had a chance to think about it, maybe you feel more reconciled to his proposition for selling the land." Tom's features were earnest. "Honestly, Cris, it's not such a bad idea. You don't want to spend the rest of your life up in this backwater. Sure, it's fine for a vacation, but that's all. I need to get back to work in civilization and I wish you'd come with me." He reached over to clasp her hand between his as she stared at him, completely bewildered by his sudden appeal.

She didn't try to escape his grip immediately, but she found herself wishing for the usual hordes of hikers around them on the trail so Tom would have postponed his entreaty. "I'm sorry," she managed finally, getting to her feet. "It just wouldn't work—between us, I mean. Otherwise it wouldn't matter about the land—or jobs—or anything."

"You haven't given me a chance. I know this isn't

the place, Cris, but—" He broke off as he gripped her chin and brought his mouth down roughly to cover hers.

Startled by his sudden move, she stayed passive in his embrace for a moment until she felt his other hand fumbling at the front of her jacket. As she stiffened in protest, he abandoned that venture but slid his arm around her waist to keep her close. "What in the devil have you got on under that jacket?" he burst out angrily, as he raised his head. "It's like trying to make love to the Abominable Snowman!"

"Snowperson, if you don't mind." Cris tried to keep a straight face and finally gave up, breaking into helpless laughter. "I'm sorry, Tom—honestly, but I couldn't resist." She sobered after noting his offended expression. "It was kind of you to try and haul my irons out of the fire. If I had any sense, I'd take you up on your offer and let Webb sell off this land without arguing. Then we could live in the sun someplace and trade all these layers of clothing for bikinis and a swimming pool."

"Exactly what I had in mind . . ."

She stopped him with a determined shake of her head. "But I can't—I simply can't. So maybe it's just as well that we're dressed this way."

"But not as much fun." There was a considering look in his eye that didn't belong to a staid accountant, and for just an instant, Cris felt a twinge of regret to match his.

"You're probably right," she said. Before he could twist that to his advantage, she reached down and swung the knapsack on her shoulder. "If I stay here any longer, I'll be frozen to the ground."

He reached for his own pack. "With all the

clothes you're wearing, you should be comfortable at forty below. Help me on with this thing, will you?"

She nodded and straightened the rope harness so he could slip his arms through it. "Want me to carry the shovel?" she asked, hoping to get his mind off the last few minutes. "The extra weight must be awkward for you."

"It doesn't matter," he said. "I'll keep it in my hand now that the trail is fairly level. How much further do we have to go?"

She nodded toward the rim of the moraine, where the outlines of a glacier could be seen. "That's where we're headed. The cave I was talking about is nearby. You can almost see the entrance from here."

"Looks like about a mile if we stay up on the ridge," Tom estimated. "Let's get this damned hike over with."

He sounded as if he'd reverted to his earlier bad temper. Considering all that had happened, it wasn't surprising, Cris decided. However, his abrupt manner didn't help ease the tension between them. She'd been cold and weary before having to cope with his emotional proposal, and now he sounded as if the prospect of spending another three or four hours together was the the last thing he wanted to do. It was just as well that she hadn't seriously considered spending the rest of her life with him.

"I asked if you were ready to go," he repeated impatiently.

"Yes, thanks. We'd better not waste any more time," she agreed. "Otherwise our lord and master will be back at the lodge before we are."

Tom gave her a startled look. "You mean Brock?"

"No, I mean Webb. How does Mr. Brock come into it?"

He ignored that. "I thought Colby was staying over in California. Where did you get the idea that he'd be back today?"

"From the great man himself. At least, that's what he said yesterday."

Tom pulled back a step or two. "You didn't tell me you saw him then."

"It wasn't an earthshaking occurrence. I guess it slipped my mind." She looked upward as she spoke, almost expecting a bolt of lightning to fork down at that monumental lie.

Her pronouncement was evidently more convincing than she thought, because Tom frowned and said thoughtfully, "I wonder why he was in such a hurry. Did you ever find out what he was going to do in California—other than report to his old lady?"

"Not really," Cris said, inwardly cringing at Tom's choice of words. "That 'old lady' is one of the people paying our salaries."

"I haven't forgotten that for one damned minute."

Her eyes widened at his vehement comment. When he made no attempt to moderate it, she gave up trying to function as a U.N. peacekeeping force and marched stolidly along the path.

It wasn't too much longer before they reached the beginning of the snow fields. The pitted surface of the moraine was dusted lightly at first, and then, as they continued to climb toward the mountain, the snow deepened to pack ice.

Or pack slush, Cris amended, as the marked trail came to an end and they moved carefully over the slippery surface toward the cave. "Stay as low as you can," she called to Tom when he started up a small ridge.

He halted abruptly. "Why? It's shorter this way," he argued.

"But not as safe. That ice could be honeycombed underneath with melt water. If you fell through"—she gestured tellingly—"you'd be mighty uncomfortable by the time you crawled out."

He looked disgruntled but came off the packed snow without further argument.

As Cris waited for him, she shaded her eyes against the icy glare and tried to ignore the colder temperature that seeped in through her clothes. Her boots didn't leak, but the surface slush caused an icing effect at the sole which penetrated within minutes.

When Tom got tired of trying to keep his balance on the slippery surface a few minutes later, he unfolded his small shovel and used it as a makeshift ice-axe. Cristina watched the maneuver thoughtfully as he strode ahead again. "Better than snow tires," he called back, clearly expecting her to keep up with him.

She tried, at first, and almost sprawled at full length over an unexpected dip in the surface. Fortunately she pulled upright but added two wet and cold hands to her list of frozen extremities. If she kept her balance, she couldn't tuck them in her jacket pockets to warm up. She gave herself a mental jab for not putting on her gloves from her knapsack before reaching the ice and started walking again.

"Is that the place?" Tom called finally, as he pulled up near the flank of the glacier and waited for her to catch up with him. He gestured toward a shadowed hole in the hillside some fifty feet away. "I thought you said it was bigger."

She came alongside and squinted toward the grimy ice. A stream of water some six to eight feet wide flowed steadily over the rocks at the base of the opening, looking like a muddy smear as it cut its way down toward the moraine. She frowned as she looked again at the cave aperture, which didn't measure more than six feet in all directions. "It's certainly smaller than I heard. Somebody told Kazy that it was a good twenty feet across about two weeks ago. I wonder if part of the snow at the entrance has already collapsed from the rain."

Tom eyed the black opening with reluctance. "We'd better go and see before we put up the sign—as long as we've come this far."

"I think we'll have to do more than that." Cris blew on her frozen fingers almost absently.

"What else is there?" This time, Tom was content to let her set the pace as they slithered along the short rise leading to the cave.

"We'll have to check the interior to make sure that there aren't any casualties already. If the snow roof has collapsed at the back of the cave and anybody was in there at the time—well, it could be bad," she finished after a moment's hesitation.

Tom didn't reply, but there was an uneasy expression on his face as they walked on, keeping their attention on the cave.

It seemed to stare back at them—a black eye surrounded by a solid wall of white, Cris fantasized. By then she was so cold that it was easier to let her mind wander than to linger on reality. The snow shelf around the shadowed aperture looked like a soiled Elizabethan ruff edged in a sawtooth pattern with the surface undercut in a graceful curve which extended some fifteen feet on either side of the entrance. The crescent looked inviting on that bleak plateau, its soft lines beckoning like a Lorelei in stern surroundings. Then, dramatically—from the mist above the glacier—the mountain suddenly emerged to add a new dimension of scenic grandeur.

Tom commented on it as he stopped for breath. "This view is just like the postcards, isn't it?" He gazed upward over the distinctive silhouette of Gibraltar Rock near the summit of Rainier. "Imagine all that snow even at this time of year. God, it makes me cold just to look at it." He stabbed the shovel down into the snow at his feet and started shouldering out of his backpack. "Let's plant this sign and then get out of here. I'll leave my cave exploring until another time. If any hikers were fool enough to go in there in the first place"—he jerked his head toward the small opening—"then they deserve whatever they got."

Cristina frowned. "Anybody would think you were related to Marie Antoinette."

"I always thought she had a lot going for her." He secured the rope harness in a neat hank and threaded it onto his belt before picking up the signpost. "Besides, without a lantern in there, you couldn't see any farther than you could spit—" He broke off as he saw her rummage in her knapsack and pull out a flashlight. "Anybody would think you were related to Houdini," he said, paraphrasing her sourly. "What else do you have in there?"

"I'd *like* to have another pair of socks." She kept her voice light. "It wouldn't do for you to go in even if you wanted to. That jacket of yours isn't waterproof."

"What does that have to do with it?"

"Caves leak," she said succinctly, gesturing toward the stream flowing from the entrance. "All that water comes from inside. The roof, the walls—the whole bundle. It's like a refrigerated rain forest."

Tom frowned as she unzipped the collar of her jacket and extracted a nylon hood which she pulled over her cap. "How long will this safari of yours last?" he asked.

"Not any longer than I can help." Cris was wishing that she'd thought to tuck a pair of nylon rain pants in the knapsack as well. The drippy cave ceiling would probably soak the legs of her slacks in no time. "I'll leave the knapsack out here and just take the flashlight with me."

"Okay. I'll put up this signpost while you're in there. Not that anybody will read it," he continued morosely, "but if they get killed, the lodge won't be responsible."

"On that cheery note, I'll leave." When she saw him look over the hillside appraisingly, she added, "For heaven's sake, don't post that thing up above the entrance. There's no telling how thin the ice is on the ceiling. If you go clambering around up there, you'll probably make the whole thing collapse."

His expression changed to alarm as her warning penetrated. "And I'd go with it?"

"That's right. We'd look like two frozen dinners by the time they dug us out."

"You've convinced me," he said, moving back a step or two from the curving ice bank by the opening. "I won't even breathe hard."

"That's the idea." She was double-checking her belongings as she spoke. "I think that's everything."

"Cris, you're sure you want to go in there?" His

voice was hesitant, as if even then he was still unsure.

"Of course. And don't drink all the rest of that coffee in my sack while I'm gone—save a swallow for me."

She turned and made her way carefully into the narrow opening, giving the snow overhang plenty of leeway. To do it, she had to wade into the center of the shallow icy stream coursing the floor of the cave. A blast of chilled air that felt as if it had come straight from the Antarctic hit her as she got past the narrow entrance. She stood blinking in the sudden gloom before shifting to the pebble-strewn edge of the stream bed. That move took care of the water seeping in her boots but it was the only improvement. Icy drops still pelted down onto her hood and shoulders from the cave ceiling in a haphazard pattern. At her side, the moisture slithering down the gray icy walls reminded her of a scaly creature shedding its skin.

Some icy drips slid under the cuff of her jacket when she reached up impatiently to mop her face. She shivered, uttered a soft "Damn!" and moved on into the cave.

It was bigger than she'd heard, bigger than she'd ever expected—making a mockery of her plans for a "once over lightly" visit. Her flashlight beam showed clearly against the wall at her side and filtered away into the Stygian gloom of the tunnel ahead. Cristina swung the light up over her head to check the ceiling and received another shower as she raised her glance to follow the beam. At least the ice looked solid. She estimated the weight hanging over her head, and shuddered. It had better be solid. If it wasn't, Tom needn't bother with a rescue attempt.

She stood there for another instant, hunched over to avoid the trickles of water as she thought about Tom's reluctance to enter the cave. He evidently didn't possess any protective qualities, but at least he could be trusted to use his head and not disturb the surface ice—if for no other reason than to avoid being involved in a cave-in himself.

Some melt water chose that moment to splash onto the end of her nose, making her walk hastily on. She kept the flashlight beam moving as she first checked a short side tunnel. Her only discovery was a squashed beer can which she retrieved with a frown before turning back toward the main chamber. She went cautiously on to flash her light into another branch tunnel barely three feet in height. At least this was the last segment to be inspected, she decided, stooping as she pointed the flashlight toward the rounded ice wall.

It looked softer than the others; enough so that she reached out to examine it and frowned when her fingers penetrated easily. It must be closer to the surface and melting faster, she thought, and jumped as a protruding piece of ice near her foot made a rumbling crack before splashing into the melt water. She was still recovering from that and chiding herself for being so nervy when she heard the rumbling vibration repeated.

For an instant she remained crouched, waiting to see another chunk float past in the stream. Then she straightened so fast that she bumped her head in the process. There was only one explanation for sounds like that; a cave-in somewhere along the tunnel behind her.

She moved as fast as she dared back into the main cavern, slipping on the water-covered rocks even as she flashed the pale beam of light into the gloom ahead of her. Each time she moved it, she was almost afraid to breathe—terrified there would be a pile of ice obstructing the passage.

But there was no change in the tunnel. It was still cold, still dark as a forgotten corner of purgatory, and still dripping like a prehistoric rain forest—just the same as before. The vibrations she'd heard must have been an avalanche up on the glacier.

Thank god, Cris breathed, unaware until then how intense her fear was. Just the thought of being entombed in that cave until Tom could dig her out would give her nightmares for a month.

She hurried on, keeping her glance down. Her hiking shoes were soaking but at least she hadn't fallen full-length into the cold melt water running steadily toward the exit.

Then she looked again where the water flowed and clutched the flashlight tighter as she turned its beam toward the ice wall above it. Even as she checked the frozen surface, the stream at its base eddied and deepened, trying to cut a new channel.

No wonder she hadn't noticed any difference in the main chamber of the cave when she first emerged. The only change that had occurred was right in front of her. As a cave-in, it didn't amount to much because the tunnel entrance had been small to start with.

Now, unfortunately—it had completely disappeared.

Chapter Ten

•◆•

Cris wasn't sure when the full impact of reaction set in. She knew that suddenly tears were running down her already wet cheeks, and she was scrabbling at that wall of wet snow like a demented creature as she shouted, "Tom! Can you hear me?" A moment later she sagged against the icy barrier when the only response was the dismal cacophony of water falling in the chamber behind her.

She was so unstrung that the flashlight slipped in her wet hands and she made a desperate grab, managing to trap it against her knees before it fell into the water. "Dear god," she muttered, clutching it thankfully. Later, and not too much later, she'd have to think about conserving the batteries, but just now the thought of existing in that black dampness was too horrible to contemplate.

She began clawing at the icy barrier and was so intent on her task that she almost dropped the flashlight again when a man shouted, "Cris! Are you in there? For god's sake, answer me!"

"I'm here—but I want out," she shrieked back.

"I'm trying. It shouldn't take long." His voice sounded nearer. "Listen to what I'm saying. I want you to stand back in case some more snow gives way when I shift this. Do you hear me?"

"I hear—but I can help dig from this side."

172

"Goddammit, do as I say!"

She straightened in amazement. That wasn't Tom's voice. Only Webb used that tone with her. She was sure of it. "Webb?" she managed to call out, sounding strange. "You're back?"

"Now what the hell do you think?"

The snap in his words brought an idiotic smile to her cold wet face. He was back and somehow—soon—everything was going to be all right.

When the first daylight came through, Cristina forgot all his instructions and rushed over to the hole. Later, she couldn't even remember how she wriggled through. She suspected that Webb caught hold of her shoulders and pulled her out like the last olive from a bottle. After that, there was no doubt in her mind about what happened. He yanked her into his arms so forcefully that her bruised ribs undoubtedly received a decided setback in their recovery.

Cris couldn't have cared less. She was ecstatic to be exactly where she was, and from the way Webb was breathing, he apparently felt the same way. She clung to his rocklike figure shamelessly and it wasn't until half a minute later that he managed to tilt her chin so that she had to look up at him. Even then, he didn't bother to talk. He simply lowered his head to kiss her in a manner that spoke volumes. The hard, possessive feel of his hands when they moved over her completed the story. If her bulky jacket and sweater bothered him, it certainly wasn't evident in his therapy.

When he finally raised his head to look down on her, she was reluctant to meet his glance. "Don't do that again," she managed to whisper. "At least, not for a while—or maybe a minute or so," and found herself caught tight again as Webb shouted with laughter.

His amusement faded, however, when Cris took a deep breath to steady herself and looked around to ask, "Where's Tom?"

"Gone," Webb replied tersely.

Her eyes were still dark with emotion. "I don't understand. Gone where?"

"He was well across the ice field heading toward the trail when we landed in the helicopter. After he admitted where you were and I discovered you were all right, I had Charles take him back to the lodge with him in the helicopter. He has orders to get him off the property today—unless you want to prefer charges."

Cris drew in a sharp breath of dismay. "You're going too fast. Why should I do anything like that?"

"Because the cave-in wasn't an accident." Webb looked as if he was having trouble controlling his anger even then. "Tom admitted that he hid the shovel in the snow before he lit out. That meant he had no plan to rescue you until he got help on the trail or arrived back at the lodge. By then, you'd have been mighty cold and wet."

Cristina swayed slightly as she thought about Tom abandoning her in that black hellhole, knowing very well that she wouldn't have survived long under those conditions.

Webb frowned as he noted her distress. He knew part of it was due to the mental shock, but a very real part was caused by her physical ordeal. "Forget about Tom," he ordered, making sure her jacket was zipped before putting a protective arm around her and pulling her close. "I promise that you won't be bothered with him again. The rest of the explanations can wait until we're back at the lodge and you've changed into dry clothes."

"That'll take a while," she said, shivering despite his efforts as she started down the icy ridge beside him. The prospect of three and a half miles over a steep, muddy trail made her want to weep.

His head lifted as the sound of an approaching helicopter shattered the quiet air of the glacier. "Not so long. Here's our transportation now." His eyes glinted with tender amusement at her relief. "We can admire the environment another time. Right now, I thought you'd prefer creature comforts like hot water and—"

"—a chance to take off these miserable boots," she cut in with vehemence.

His clasp tightened for a moment before he guided her toward the settling 'copter. "Stick around," he promised. "In fifteen minutes, I'll even do it for you."

He did, too. Almost as soon as they reached the chalet after the helicopter put them down in a vacant corner of the parking lot.

"Mr. Brock will have a fit when he hears what's going on," Cris murmured, once the chalet door was shut behind them.

"Mr. Brock was so delighted to hear his contract is being renewed that we could fill the parking lot with helicopters three times a day and twice on Sundays," Webb corrected. "Now sit down in that chair and let me take those boots off. Without arguing," he added when she hesitated. "Then I'll turn on your bath water and after that, it's up to you. If you think you can manage. Otherwise . . ."

"I can manage, thank you," she said hastily, seeing the wicked twinkle in his eyes.

"Obviously you're getting back to normal," he commented. Even so, he didn't waste any time pulling off her soaking boots and the thick socks which were clammy with cold. Afterward she was bundled into the bathroom and deposited on a hamper while he reached over to run water into the tub. "Now I'll go find some food," he said, when he straightened and moved over to the door. "I don't know about you, but I don't believe I've eaten since last month."

"Wait, Webb!" When he looked back over his shoulder, she said, "I'll need something to wear afterward—"

He cut in before she could finish. "I'll toss your clothes around the door later on. Now get in that bath or a winding sheet is the only thing you'll be wearing in the future."

Five minutes later, Cris was luxuriating in a steaming tub full of bubbles when his arm came around the door to drop a robe and slippers just inside. "Coffee's ready when you are," he reported from the hall, and she heard his footsteps go back toward the kitchen.

When she reluctantly got out of the tub and toweled herself dry, she surveyed his offering dubiously. Why hadn't she thought about clean underthings as well? Then she decided the floor-length robe of viyella with its shawl collar and long sleeves was modest enough if she kept it tightly belted. A few minutes later with her hair combed and a touch of lipstick, she walked shyly into the kitchen.

Webb took one look at her and nodded approvingly before he ushered her over to a plate of toast and scrambled eggs. "Food first."

"Before you start explaining?"

"That and other things," he replied obliquely and picked up his own fork.

But afterward, when she was installed on the long davenport in front of a crackling fireplace fire with a second mug of coffee at her elbow, he didn't prolong her agony. "The trouble all along was that too many things were going wrong here at the lodge. That's where Tom and the people in the development company who hired him made their mistake." Webb sat down beside her and stretched his long legs out to enjoy the warmth of the blaze. "Your grandfather wasn't the only one who was concerned about the problems," he added gently. "My mother felt the same way. That's why I was recruited to come and check things out as soon as I had a week free. When I learned that Charles was working in this area, I thought we could use his knowhow, as well."

"Plus helping to patch up his trouble with Sheila," Cris put in.

Webb reddened slightly but he nodded. "That, too. Although she provided complications I hadn't counted on."

Cris remembered her own distinctly feline reaction at the time and squirmed uneasily.

Webb grinned as he noticed her discomfort. "I think we'd better call that part of our relationship a draw. Let's forget about it, shall we?"

"I wish you would."

Her fervent agreement evidently amused him, but he continued with his story. "Well, I still had nothing to go on but suspicion until the other day when Charles thought he saw Tom putting those saplings across Myrtle Creek to dam the current. Charles hung around until the coast was clear and then dragged them up on the bank. He stayed in the area to make sure there wasn't any more mischief. Later that night, he reported to me."

"And Tom said he'd been in the lakes sector that day for an alibi," she mused. "I should have suspected when he didn't know about the damage on the trail there. All he could talk about was potholes." She turned to face Webb more squarely. "I can understand an attempt to lessen the property value, but I don't understand how he could rationalize starting that fire in the annex. Something terrible could have happened if the alarm hadn't worked. And today—why did he try and hurt me?"

"I don't think he planned to when he started out from the lodge," Webb said.

Cristina absently fingered the edge of her robe as she thought about Tom's proposal earlier on the trail, and she wondered what he would have done if her answer had been different. "I don't want to prefer charges against him," she said after a while. "Even if I did, there's no real evidence."

"That's the damnable part of it," Webb agreed. He added another log to the fire and congratulated himself in the interval that she'd never know how reluctant Warden had been to admit where Cris could be found when they'd discovered him on the moraine. It had taken a black eye and a split lip to finally persuade him, but Webb didn't intend to mention that. "The whole maneuver was just business as far as Tom was concerned. He admitted it. You wouldn't sell, and he was convinced that his associates would have an easier time of obtaining the property if they just had to deal with me. I learned some of the background when I was in San Francisco." Webb shook his head wearily. "Brock wasn't supposed to let you out of sight until

I got back. Unfortunately, Tom saw the cave report as a way to get you off alone. Thank god, Yoshi noticed you on the way out of the lodge and Kazy reported that he'd seen you join Tom and start up the ice caves trail. That's when I phoned for the helicopter."

"So that's why Tom wanted me to leave at the crack of dawn," she said, remembering his phone call.

"I suppose so," Webb grimaced ruefully. "I'd made a big pitch about selling the property when we were up at Myrtle Creek so that he'd sit tight while I was away."

"Then you don't really want to sell?" Cris asked, latching on to the vital part of his comment.

"Hell no!" He grinned again. "My mother's as stubborn about this place as you are. Fortunately my stepfather's able to finance her mistakes, and I think I can indulge yours. Don't get your dander up," he said, seeing a dangerous glint in the glance Cris leveled at him. "It'll be strictly a family affair." She was still digesting that when he stood up and took the empty coffee mugs to the kitchen.

She got to her feet and came hesitantly around the end of the davenport. Feminine pride went out the window as she gave him an anxious look. "You're—you're not going, are you?"

He lounged against the end of the kitchen counter and folded his arms over his chest. "Damn right I am." She didn't have time to do more than wince before he went on roughly, "Look, my adorable but misguided idiot—I know better than to spend another night under the same roof with you, at least until we occupy the same bed." He jerked his head toward the loft but stayed where he was.

Almost, she thought giddily, as if he thought it would be safer that way.

Webb's voice deepened. "When I was home, I applied for a marriage license and my folks said that all I had to do was bring you back with me. They're fixing everything for a ceremony the day after tomorrow." He saw Cristina's gray-green eyes widen in utter bewilderment and hurried on before she could speak. "I've arranged for the copter to take us to the airport in Seattle to connect with a flight south two hours from now. I made reservations on that when I got in this morning. We can come back here for our honeymoon if you'd like. I could use some hiking pointers on the trails around the lodge," he added with a crooked smile.

She had trouble looking severe when her heart was pounding so hard that she could hardly hear over the tumult. "I'll overlook that, Mr. Colby."

"Is that all you have to say?" His own voice was uneven as he saw how happiness illuminated her face, making it lovely beyond belief.

She shook her head weakly, although she hadn't had one logical thought since he'd proposed. "I can't get married just like that. I—I don't have any proper clothes to wear."

"I don't think that's a problem on honeymoons," he assured her solemnly. "It sure as hell won't be on ours. Anything else that's bothering you?"

"Just one thing . . ."

Her tremulous appeal broke the bonds of restraint Webb had imposed with such difficulty. He took three strides and caught her in a tender possessive embrace. "Darling Cris," he murmured with his lips brushing her temple and nuzzling the top of her ear. "Would it help if I told you how much I love you—how I've been looking for you all my life? I knew the minute I saw you leaning over the lodge railing that you were meant for me. From now on, I'm keeping you close, where you belong!"

His hands moved urgently then—down over her back to her hips as his mouth parted hers. Pressed close against his tall form, Cris returned his caresses, acknowledging that her need matched his. Then the banked-down fire of desire flamed high between them as she surrendered unreservedly to his demands.

"*Now* do you see why I want to get that plane?" Webb's tone was rough with emotion as he reluctantly moved away from her some minutes later.

She looked up at him and managed to nod, still breathing hard as her hands tightened the belt on her robe.

For a moment, she wished that time would stand still. Just at that instant when Webb's disturbing glance showed how much he wanted her and reflected the love they shared. He'd caused utter havoc in her heart from the very beginning. Now, it seemed, she was promised that sheer heaven for the rest of her life.

Webb drew in his breath sharply as he saw the shy radiance of her smile, but he forced himself to stand motionless—waiting until she said,

"Please help me pack, Webb, dearest. And hurry, will you—we have a plane to catch."

About the Author

Glenna Finley is a native of Washington State. She earned her degree from Stanford University in Russian Studies and in Speech and Dramatic Arts, with emphasis on radio.

After a stint in radio and publicity work in Seattle, she went to New York City to work for NBC as a producer in its international division. In addition, she worked with the "March of Time" and *Life* magazine.

As a producer, she had her own show about activities in Manhattan, a show that was broadcast to England. The programs were similar to those of the "Voice of America."

Though her life in New York was exciting, she eventually returned to the Northwest where she married. Currently residing in Seattle with her husband, Donald Witte, and their son, she loves to travel, and draws heavily on her travels and experiences for the novels that have been published. Her books for NAL have sold several million copies.

Big Bestsellers from SIGNET

☐ **THE SILVER FALCON by Evelyn Anthony.**
(#E8211—$2.25)

☐ **I, JUDAS by Taylor Caldwell and Jess Stearn.**
(#E8212—$2.50)

☐ **THE RAGING WINDS OF HEAVEN by June Shiplett.**
(#J8213—$1.95)*

☐ **THE SERGEANT MAJOR'S DAUGHTER by Sheila Walsh.**
(#E8220—$1.75)

☐ **I CAME TO THE HIGHLANDS by Velda Johnston.**
(#J8218—$1.95)*

☐ **THE TODAY SHOW by Robert Metz.** (#E8214—$2.25)

☐ **HEAT by Arthur Herzog.** (#J8115—$1.95)*

☐ **THE SWARM by Arthur Herzog.** (#E8079—$2.25)

☐ **BLOCKBUSTER by Stephen Barlay.** (#E8111—$2.25)*

☐ **SHADOW OF A BROKEN MAN by George Chesbro.**
(#J8114—$1.95)*

☐ **BORN TO WIN by Muriel James and Dorothy Jongeward.**
(#E8169—$2.50)*

☐ **THE LADY SERENA by Jeanne Duval.**
(#E8163—$2.25)*

☐ **BORROWED PLUMES by Roseleen Milne.**
(#E8113—$1.75)

☐ **LOVING STRANGERS by Jack Mayfield.**
(#J8216—$1.95)*

☐ **BALLET! by Tom Murphy.** (#E8112—$2.25)*

☐ **ROGUE'S MISTRESS by Constance Gluyas.**
(#E8339—$2.25)

☐ **SAVAGE EDEN by Constance Gluyas.** (#E8338—$2.25)

☐ **WOMAN OF FURY by Constance Gluyas.**
(#E8075—$2.25)*

☐ **BEYOND THE MALE MYTH by Anthony Pietropinto, M.D.,
and Jacqueline Simenauer.** (#E8076—$2.50)

☐ **CRAZY LOVE: An Autobiographical Account of Marriage
and Madness by Phyllis Naylor.** (#J8077—$1.95)

*Price slightly higher in Canada

More Big Bestsellers from SIGNET

☐ **THE PSYCHOPATHIC GOD: ADOLF HITLER** by Robert G. L. Waite. (#E8078—$2.95)

☐ **THE SERIAL** by Cyra McFadden. (#J8080—$1.95)

☐ **TWINS** by Bari Wood and Jack Geasland. (#E8015—$2.50)

☐ **MARATHON: The Pursuit of the Presidency 1972-1976** by Jules Witcover. (#E8034—$2.95)

☐ **THE RULING PASSION** by Shaun Herron. (#E8042—$2.25)

☐ **CONSTANTINE CAY** by Catherine Dillon. (#J8307—$1.95)

☐ **WHITE FIRES BURNING** by Catherine Dillon. (#J8281—$1.95)

☐ **THE WHITE KHAN** by Catherine Dillon. (#J8043—$1.95)*

☐ **DAMIEN—OMEN II** by Joseph Howard. (#J8164—$1.95)

☐ **THE OMEN** by David Seltzer. (#J8180—$1.95)

☐ **KID ANDREW CODY AND JULIE SPARROW** by Tony Curtis. (#E8010—$2.25)*

☐ **WINTER FIRE** by Susannah Leigh. (#E8011—$2.25)*

☐ **THE MESSENGER** by Mona Williams. (#J8012—$1.95)

☐ **FEAR OF FLYING** by Erica Jong. (#E7970—$2.25)

☐ **HOW TO SAVE YOUR OWN LIFE** by Erica Jong. (#E7959—$2.50)*

☐ **HARVEST OF DESIRE** by Rochelle Larkin. (#E8183—$2.25)

☐ **MISTRESS OF DESIRE** by Rochelle Larkin. (#E7964—$2.25)*

☐ **THE FIRES OF GLENLOCHY** by Constance Heaven. (#E7452—$1.75)

☐ **THE PLACE OF STONES** by Constance Heaven. (#W7046—$1.50)

☐ **THE QUEEN AND THE GYPSY** by Constance Heaven. (#J7965—$1.95)

*Price slightly higher in Canada

Have You Read These Bestsellers from SIGNET?

☐ **TORCH SONG by Anne Roiphe.**   (#J7901—$1.95)

☐ **OPERATION URANIUM SHIP by Dennis Eisenberg, Eli Landau, and Menanem Portugali.**   (#E8001—$1.75)

☐ **NIXON VS. NIXON by Dr. David Abrahamsen.**
(#E7902—$2.25)

☐ **ISLAND OF THE WINDS by Athena Dallas-Damis.**
(#J/905—$1.95)

☐ **CARRIE by Stephen King.**   (#J7280—$1.95)

☐ **'SALEM'S LOT by Stephen King.**   (#E8000—$2.25)

☐ **THE SHINING by Stephen King.**   (#E7872—$2.50)

☐ **OAKHURST by Walter Reed Johnson.** (#J7874—$1.95)

☐ **FRENCH KISS by Mark Logan.**   (#J7876—$1.95)

☐ **COMA by Robin Cook.**   (#E8202—$2.50)

☐ **CARIBEE by Christopher Nicole.**   (#J7945—$1.95)

☐ **THE DEVIL'S OWN by Christopher Nicole.**
(#J7256—$1.95)

☐ **MISTRESS OF DARKNESS by Christopher Nicole.**
(#J7782—$1.95)

☐ **DESIRES OF THY HEART by Joan Carroll Cruz.**
(#J7738—$1.95)

☐ **CALDO LARGO by Earl Thompson.**   (#E7737—$2.25)

☐ **A GARDEN OF SAND by Earl Thompson.**
(#E8039—$2.50)

☐ **TATTOO by Earl Thompson.**   (#E8038—$2.50)

☐ **THE ACCURSED by Paul Boorstin.**   (#E7745—$1.75)

☐ **THE RICH ARE WITH YOU ALWAYS by Malcolm Macdonald.**   (#E7682—$2.25)

☐ **THE WORLD FROM ROUGH STONES by Malcolm Macdonald.**   (#J6891—$1.95)

NAL/ABRAMS' BOOKS
ON ART, CRAFTS AND SPORTS
in beautiful, large format, special concise editions—lavishly illustrated with many full-color plates.

☐ **THE ART OF WALT DISNEY: From Mickey Mouse to the Magic Kingdoms** by Christopher Finch. (#G9982—$7.95)

☐ **DISNEY'S AMERICA ON PARADE: A History of the U.S.A. in a Dazzling, Fun-Filled Pageant,** text by David Jacobs. (#G9974—$7.95)

☐ **FREDERIC REMINGTON** by Peter Hassrick. (#G9980—$6.95)

☐ **GRANDMA MOSES** by Otto Kallir. (#G9981—$6.95)

☐ **THE POSTER IN HISTORY** by Max Gallo. (#G9976—$7.95)

☐ **THE SCIENCE FICTION BOOK: An Illustrated History** by Franz Rottensteiner. (#G9978—$6.95)

☐ **NORMAN ROCKWELL: A Sixty Year Retrospective** by Thomas S. Buechner. (#G9969—$7.95)

☐ **MUHAMMAD ALI** by Wilfrid Sheed. (#G9977—$7.95)

☐ **THE PRO FOOTBALL EXPERIENCE** edited by David Boss, with an Introduction by Roger Kahn. (#G9984—$6.95)

☐ **THE DOLL** text by Carl Fox, photographs by H. Landshoff. (#G9987—$5.95)

☐ **DALI . . . DALI . . . DALI . . .** edited and arranged by Max Gérard. (#G9983—$6.95)

☐ **THOMAS HART BENTON** by Matthew Baigell. (#G9979—$6.95)

☐ **THE WORLD OF M. C. ESCHER** by M. C. Escher and J. L. Locher. (#G9970—$7.95)
